THE WONDROUS WORLD OF
VIOLET BARNABY

THE WONDROUS WORLD OF VIOLET BARNABY

JENNY LUNDQUIST

WITHDRAWN

Aladdin

New York London Toronto Sydney New Delhi

This book is a work of fiction. Any references to historical events, real people, or real places are used fictitiously. Other names, characters, places, and events are products of the author's imagination, and any resemblance to actual events or places or persons, living or dead, is entirely coincidental.

ALADDIN

An imprint of Simon & Schuster Children's Publishing Division

1230 Avenue of the Americas, New York, New York 10020

First Aladdin paperback edition September 2017

Text copyright © 2017 by Jenny Lundquist

Cover illustration copyright © 2017 by Ilaria Falorsi

Also available in an Aladdin hardcover edition.

All rights reserved, including the right of reproduction in whole or in part in any form.

ALADDIN and related logo are registered trademarks of Simon & Schuster, Inc.

For information about special discounts for bulk purchases, please contact

Simon & Schuster Special Sales at 1-866-506-1949 or business@simonandschuster.com.

The Simon & Schuster Speakers Bureau can bring authors to your live event.

For more information or to book an event contact the Simon & Schuster Speakers Bureau at 1-866-248-3049 or visit our website at www.simonspeakers.com.

Cover designed by Jessica Handelman

Interior designed by Mike Rosamilia

The text of this book was set in Dante MT.

Manufactured in the United States of America

0817 OFF

2 4 6 8 10 9 7 5 3 1

Library of Congress Control Number: 2017946535

ISBN 978-1-4814-6035-4 (hc)

ISBN 978-1-4814-6034-7 (pbk)

ISBN 978-1-4814-6036-1 (eBook)

To Finnigan Joseph and Graysun Monet,
the two of you make the world a more wondrous place

CONTENTS

CHAPTER
1

SHABBY SWEAT-SHIRTS

I have a glittery purple journal where I keep word lists. Each list has a different title, like Words I Love, Funny Words, or Words That Annoy Me. On my list of Words I Love, I have "sparkling," "bubbling," and "spinning" because they remind me of parties and people smiling and no tears at all. It's my favorite list. But it's been a long time since I added anything to it.

I also have a list of Words I Don't Like. Words like "bucolic," which means "relating to rural life," but reminds me of the flu, and makes me queasy every time I hear it. Then there are words I despise, words that can wrap around your heart and squeeze you until you feel like you can't breathe anymore.

For my dad and me, that word is "cancer."

"Cancer"—It's on the top of my Words I Hate list. But last month, I added a new word just below it:

"Stepmother."

For Halloween most kids got a bucketful of candy. I got a stepmother. And not just any stepmother, either. Nope. My dad couldn't meet a nice lady over the Internet like a normal person. No, he had to go and marry Ms. Melanie Harmer—aka the Hammer—the meanest teacher at Dandelion Middle School.

Dad and Melanie got engaged at the end of October, but they didn't want the hassle of a long engagement. So while other kids were putting away their Halloween costumes and trading candy with their friends, I was putting on my old Easter dress and trying not to puke the whole way over to the county courthouse, where it took the judge less than ten minutes to pronounce Dad and Melanie man and wife.

As I stood there, watching them kiss, I wondered what it would be like to live with the Hammer and her two kids—Olivia, who's my age; and Joey, who's eight—in the house Dad and Melanie bought.

Now, nearly a month later, it was the Saturday after Thanksgiving. Moving Day. Dad and I were in Dad's soon-to-be-vacated bedroom. The moving people had taken almost everything out of the house. We had just a few things to pack up before we left the only house I'd ever lived in forever. With all the furniture gone, it didn't seem like a real home anymore. Of course, it hadn't felt like a real home for the last year and a half, since Mom died.

I swept the floor while Dad went through a box of old clothes. Once I finished with the broom I checked "Sweep Dad's Floor" off the cleaning list I'd made. The list was two pages long, but I was almost finished with it. Dad wanted the house to be spotless before he gave the keys to his real estate agent.

Dad held up a green T-shirt. "What do you think? Keep or toss?"

"Toss, definitely," I said. "It has holes in the sleeves."

Dad stared at it and frowned. "I guess. But I could find a use for it. Maybe when I paint?"

"Dad, we talked about this," I reminded him. "Toss it."

"Okay, okay." Dad moved it into the trash pile, and then pulled out a raggedy sweatshirt. "What about this one?"

"Mom gave you that one, remember?" I said.

Dad flushed, and hurriedly put it into his "for keeps" pile, muttering that he was sorry, and I felt like a big jerk. The sweatshirt was really shabby and falling apart, and it's not like I thought that by throwing it out he was forgetting Mom. But sometimes I feel like he's packed up and moved into Melanie's life and left me behind. Like *I'm* an old sweatshirt that suddenly seems too small and too shabby. Maybe one day Dad had woken up and decided he'd outgrown his old life. Our life. Then he met Melanie.

While Dad finished going through the box, I consulted my list. Next up was "Vacuum Your Room," so I headed for my bedroom. I paused in the empty living room. Memories of my mom filled these rooms and they spun around me like dust motes dancing in the sunlight. I wondered if the new owners would know how happy our family had been here—before Mom got sick, that is. Would they know she used to sit by the fireplace and knit, or that there used to be a piano under the window where her music students would play during their afternoon lessons, or that next to that piano was a vintage record player where we played old records from her collection—always records, never a CD or an iPod, because she felt a true fan of music should have a decent record collection?

But now that piano was at my friend Izzy's house so

her sister Carolyn could use it, and our record collection, along with the rest of our furniture, was packed up and on its way to the new house—or on its way to the Goodwill, because Melanie said we no longer needed it.

My room didn't look like a real bedroom anymore, either. I stared at the purple walls as I ran the vacuum cleaner. Mom and I had painted them together; she'd even let me stay home from school one day to do it. A couple days later, after the paint had dried, she sat me down on my bed, and said, "I have something to tell you."

It's amazing how quickly six little words can change your entire life.

Next on my list was: "Wipe Down Dad's Closet."

I pulled a paint-splattered folding chair up to the top shelf and was about to get started when I saw a dusty red envelope pushed against the corner. I flipped it over. On the outside it read, "For Violet, For Christmas." I recognized the handwriting immediately.

It was my mother's.

CHAPTER 2

MEMORIES THAT WON'T GET MADE

"Dad! Dad, come in here!"

I must have sounded pretty panicky, because Dad came rushing in. His cell phone was ringing. By the ringtone—a shrill-sounding trumpet—I knew it was Melanie calling again. Apparently, the movers Dad had hired were completely incompetent, and for some reason she needed to call him every ten minutes to tell him so.

"What?" he said as he sent the call to voice mail. "What is it?" His face turned white when he saw the envelope. "Where did you get that?"

"I found it in your closet."

We stared at the letter, and Mom's swooping cursive,

until Dad sank onto the folding chair, and put his head in his hands. "I'm so sorry," he said, his voice sounding muffled. "I forgot—" His phone trumpeted. With an irritated grunt, he sent the call to voice mail again. "I completely forgot about that letter. I was supposed to have given it to you *last* December, but . . ."

He trailed off, but I understood. Last Christmas—Black Christmas, I called it privately—was our first one without Mom, and Dad had forgotten a lot of things. To put up a tree. To buy presents. To buy groceries. Sometimes it seemed like he even forgot I was in the room.

"Do you remember all those letters Mom wrote you when you were having trouble with spelling?" he asked.

I nodded. Mom used to write me long letters, using all the words on my spelling list. It was the highlight of the week for me, getting her notes. Pretty soon, I became the best speller in my class.

"Well . . . before she died, she wrote you a letter. She thought the holiday season might be hard for you. You know how much she loved Christmas."

I nodded again, but I hoped he wouldn't go into a big pep talk about holiday cheer. I had no interest in Christmas, or the holiday season at all. It was fine with me if we just skipped straight ahead to New Year's.

"I'm so sorry," Dad said. "I really didn't mean—" His phone rang again and he muttered a nasty word under his breath.

"You'd probably better answer it," I said. "She'll just keep calling."

"I'll text her." While Dad tapped on his phone, I stared at the letter, my heart pounding.

When someone you love dies, no one ever tells you that you've lost more than just that person. You've lost a lifetime of memories that won't get made. You've lost a lifetime of getting to hear that person's voice. But here in this letter were Mom's words, and I was sure when I read them, I'd hear her voice. A voice I missed so much I oftentimes felt sick inside.

"Do you want to read it now?" Dad asked. "Before . . ."

Before we go to the new house is what he meant. Melanie's house, a place Mom would never be.

Dad's cell pinged with a text, and we both glanced at the message: I NEED YOU HERE TO DIRECT THE MOVERS. THEY'RE IDIOTS!

"It's okay," I said. "I can read it later."

I shoved the letter into my backpack. As much as I wanted to tear it right open, I wanted to do it on my own time. When Melanie wasn't interrupting every two seconds—like a shrill alarm clock you just couldn't shut off.

CHAPTER
3

A NEW START

As Dad started up the car, I looked at our house one last time. The front door was made of worn, splintered wood and was painted a bright shade of red that Mom always said reminded her of ripe strawberries. The door got smaller and smaller as we drove down the street, until we turned the corner and it slipped from view altogether.

Here's something else that's red and worn and splintered: a heart that's been broken in two.

We were only moving to the next neighborhood over, but it felt like a million miles away, and my stomach heaved when the new house came into view. It was a big two-story that was painted brown with bright white shutters and trim. It also had a huge wraparound porch and a big bay window. It was exactly the kind of house Mom said she wanted to live in one day.

"Ready, Champ?" Dad asked as he shut the car off. He started calling me Champ after I'd won the fourth-grade spelling bee, and the name stuck. He was smiling, and as much as I didn't like Ms. Harm—Melanie—I at least appreciated that. Smiling Dad was much better than Crying Dad. Of course, he only ever cried at night, when he thought I was sleeping.

"I'm ready," I lied. "Let's go."

As we strode up the walkway, I ran my fingers along the golden charm bracelet I always wear on my wrist, and I felt a little better. My friends Izzy, Sophia, and Daisy have the same bracelet, and I was going to see them tomorrow night at the Dandelion Hollow Christmas-Tree-Lighting.

I just had to get through the next day and a half first.

The front yard was covered in boxes, and Melanie was arguing with one of the movers—a short, round man whose eyebrows looked like thick black slugs.

"What's going on?" Dad asked.

"The movers are quitting," Melanie said, shooting the man a withering glare.

"We're not quitting," he said, going red in the face. "I

just refuse to have my men continually berated because you couldn't be bothered to label your boxes."

"The boxes *are* labeled!" Melanie shouted.

"Where?" He spread his hands wide. "Show me, and my men will get back to work. Otherwise, we're leaving. We're not waiting around while you open every single box!"

"They were labeled!" Melanie insisted. "I don't know what happened!" Her eyes found mine. "Do you know anything about this?" she demanded.

I wanted so badly to say something snarky back to her. But Mom always said, "If you can't say something nice, it's better to say nothing at all." Consequently, I've spent a lot of the last month keeping my mouth shut.

"No, I just got here," I said, in a polite voice. *Not nearly enough time to screw anything up for you*, I added silently in a decidedly not-polite voice. Melanie had been irritated with me all week. All month, actually, ever since Dad had let her into our house and the two of them had started deciding what to keep and what they should donate. I overheard her in the kitchen telling Dad she "didn't appreciate my attitude" when they'd taken Joey, Olivia, and me to the new house to pick out our new bedrooms. I'd wanted to go marching in there and ask why I should be excited about it; none of the rooms in the new house were as good as the one she was making me leave behind.

The movers started packing up, and Melanie went scurrying after them. Dad scratched his head. "That's strange. I know we labeled them. Well . . . I guess we'd better get them all off the yard."

Dad picked up a box and headed inside. I grabbed one and nearly toppled over—it must have weighed a ton. Olivia, who'd been sitting on a rocker on the front porch while all of this was happening, said, "Careful, that one's heavy."

"Thanks for the tip," I snapped, dropping the box.

"Excuse me?" A deliveryman carrying a stack of pizzas came striding up to us. "I've got a delivery for a Mrs. Barnaby—is that your mother?"

"No," Olivia said, just as I answered, "Yes."

We glanced at each other and blinked. I realized he was talking about Melanie, not Mom. It made me sick that I had the same last name as the Hammer now—but at least she hadn't changed it yet at Dandelion Middle.

"I mean, yes, that's my mother," Olivia said, just as I said, "No."

The deliveryman sighed like he didn't have time for our nonsense. "Are you two sisters?"

"No," Olivia answered.

"Definitely not," I said.

"My mom's in the garage with the movers, I think," Olivia added.

"Yeah, just listen for the sound of shrill arguing, and you'll find her," I said.

The deliveryman sighed again and started for the garage. Olivia shot me a murderous look. Forget being sisters—Olivia and I weren't even friends. I'd met her for the first time last summer, not too long after Dad and Melanie started dating. I think since we were both starting sixth grade at Dandelion Middle, Melanie thought we'd become BFFs or something.

"Want to eat lunch together in the cafeteria?" Olivia had asked me the night before school started. She sounded about as excited as someone getting their tooth pulled, and I was pretty sure Melanie had put her up to it.

"I'm busy," I'd answered.

"Busy doing what?"

"I don't know yet," I'd said. "I just know I'm busy."

After that, we pretty much went out of our way to ignore each other at school.

I picked up a couple small boxes, and Olivia, still lounging on the porch, said, "Those belong in the living room."

"Way to be helpful," I said, and headed for the house.

Inside it smelled like disinfectant, and furniture was haphazardly pushed up against the walls. Half-opened boxes littered the floor. In the middle of the living room was a huge box of Melanie's Christmas decorations. I wanted to stomp all over them until they broke into tiny bits—she'd decided that Mom and Dad's decorations were too old and worn, so she sent most of them off to the Goodwill.

From the front door I heard Melanie shriek, "Who tracked mud into the house?"

I looked down at my tennis shoes. Oops.

"Those are Violet's footprints," Olivia was saying to Melanie, who was now carrying the stack of pizzas, when I reached the entryway. "She moved some boxes into the house."

"Because you *told* me to," I said.

"Um, hello? I didn't think I'd have to tell you to wipe your feet first. What are you, five? Why don't you go and 'help' somewhere else?" she said, making air quotes around the word "help."

"Fine—I've got better things to do, anyway," I said, thinking of Mom's letter.

"Olivia, cool it," Melanie warned as Dad joined us. "The mud will come out." To me, she said, "How was your drive over?" Like we'd taken a trip across the country, instead of a short ride across Thistle Street. Dad put his hand on my back, and I knew I had to answer nicely.

"It was fine. I'm going to miss my old room, though."

Melanie flushed, and Dad squeezed my shoulder, like I'd said something wrong, instead of just answering truthfully. Melanie asked Olivia to put the pizzas in the kitchen; then she led Dad and me upstairs, making chirpy comments about the house, and when she reached my new room she threw open the door, and said, "Isn't it great?"

I just smiled and nodded. Because if I was honest, the room was terrible; it looked even worse than I remembered. My mattress lay on the floor. A pile of boxes was stacked in the center—making the room look smaller than it already was. The walls were white and dusty, and the window was grimy.

It just didn't seem like someplace I could ever call my own.

Dad was smiling and staring at me expectantly. I searched for something nice to say: "These walls would look great in purple." I could already imagine it, and I knew Izzy would help me paint. She doesn't like boring walls, either. Last month, she got into a ton of trouble for painting a wall at school orange. Well, *we* got into a ton of trouble, because I helped her do it.

"Purple?" Melanie blinked, and chewed on her cheek. Sometimes when she does that, she looks like she's swallowing her lips.

"Yeah, I think I'll paint them purple. Just like my old room."

"I wasn't aware we were painting the walls," Melanie said, glancing at Dad, who suddenly looked uncomfortable.

Dad shifted back and forth, and I could tell he wished I hadn't said anything. "We'll have to figure it out later, won't we, Champ?" His smile dimmed, and more than anything else, I didn't want him to stop smiling.

"Dad never said I could paint the walls," I said quickly. "It's just, I painted my other room, and I guess I just assumed . . ."

"Well," Melanie said with forced cheerfulness, "we're all making a new start, aren't we? We'll talk about paint later."

"Sure," I said.

But I knew I'd be stuck with white walls for a long time.

4

THE TERRIBLE
BEAUTIFUL ACHE

After Dad and Melanie left, the door to my closet sprang open, and a small voice said, "Are they gone?"

I jumped and nearly tripped over a box as Joey stepped into the room. As far as stepbrothers go, Joey isn't too bad. He's short with flyaway blond hair and black plastic glasses that make his blue eyes seem twice as large.

"Yeah, they're gone," I answered, kicking the box out of my way. "And what were you doing in there, anyway?"

"I'm hiding, and your closet is bigger than mine," he said, plopping down on my mattress. "Have you ever heard of a spy kit?"

"No," I said, moving a half-opened box of books off my mattress. Odd—the box was blank, but I *knew* I'd labeled it yesterday.

"I got one for my birthday," Joey continued. "And it came with a bunch of spy pens. They have disappearing ink, and I think I accidentally got them mixed up with—"

"With the pens everyone used for packing," I finished, solving the mystery of the suddenly not labeled boxes.

Joey nodded. "I'm sure Mom will figure it out soon, and she says it's naughty if I don't come when she calls, so I'm trying to find a place where I can't hear her." He stared at me seriously. "And that's hard because she has a really loud voice."

I had to laugh at that. Beneath Joey's cherub good looks lurked a criminal mastermind in the making. "What about in the backyard?" I said. "I bet you couldn't hear her out there."

His eyes widened. "That's brilliant!" We high-fived, and after he scampered off, I shut the door behind him. Then I sat on my mattress, and pulled out Mom's letter from my backpack. I stared at it for a while before taking a deep breath and opening it. My mouth felt dry and my hands shook as I read:

Dear Violet,

I hope that you are happy to be getting a letter from me. But if you aren't, if this is too much, put this away right now and don't open it again until you're ready and the time is right.

I'm in the Kaleidoscope Café as I write this. Dad and I just got finished with another doctor's appointment, and the clock tells me it's after ten in the morning. When I was younger, Time was something I strained against, because it seemed to move so slowly, like trying to swim through a pool of orange marmalade. Now that I'm older, Time feels more like a bullet train zooming along, and I wish I had more of it. Because the truth is, the doctors say I don't have a lot of time left. The trees outside are sparkling with sunlight and the Kaleidoscope smells like cinnamon pancakes. "Kaleidoscope," I love that word. I wonder if you have it on your list of Words I Love? The thing that interests me about kaleidoscopes is that you can be looking at a beautiful scene, and if you shift things around ever so slightly, the picture will *completely change and everything will look totally different.*

I know that's how it's going to feel after I'm gone. Like everything has shifted around and is unrecognizable.

And I know that hurts, Violet. But I'm here to tell you, it's possible to find beauty in the new pattern, even if you're missing me. I promise that one day missing me will get easier. I learned that after my own mom died, your grandma Gayle. It's sort of like a splinter that's buried deep in your heart. Some days you feel the ache more than others, but it's always there, and although the pain gets easier to bear, it never completely goes away. I call it the Terrible Beautiful Ache.

Terrible, because it's a pain you wouldn't wish on anyone; but beautiful, because you've discovered exactly how precious life is, and that's a lesson many people don't learn until they're much older. I wish you didn't have to experience the Terrible Beautiful Ache so young, Violet. Some things in life are just not fair.

While I was writing this, someone came into the café and was talking about Christmas, and it occurred to me that this Christmas, your first without me, is going to be pretty hard. I know Christmas is supposed to be a time of happiness and joy. But I also know that every year, no matter how old I got, I missed my mom. That's what I want you to know, Violet. It's okay to miss me. It's okay to always miss me. I know you, Violet. You are a girl who feels things deeply, and I don't want you to be embarrassed about that. But I also want you to know that it's okay to enjoy this season, too, to make memories, and have good times. I want you to know that it's possible to do that, even while you're missing me. Nothing would make me happier than to know you were enjoying this holiday season, and I have decided to help you do it! You've never met a list you couldn't conquer, so with this letter I'm including your Christmas To-Do List. It's a list of things I hope you'll do this season to make some happy memories. While you're doing them, picture me smiling at you and cheering you on.

Love always,
Mom

By the time I'd finished reading, my heart was pounding fast. Mom's voice sounded as warm and comforting as a cup of tea and a roaring fire on a rainy day. I cradled the letter in my hands, because I knew it was rare and precious, and probably the best present I'd ever receive in my life. I read it again and again; until an ache—the Terrible Beautiful Ache, I guess—squeezed my heart so much I had to put it aside and look at the list on the second page:

Violet's Christmas To-Do List!

- Roast marshmallows in the fire pit
- String popcorn garland
- Volunteer for a good cause
- Buy a gift for someone important
- Attend Dandelion Hollow's Christmas tree-lighting
- Play a Christmas game
- Watch Christmas movies
- Sing carols
- Go sledding
- Bake Christmas cookies
- Make snow angels
- Decorate a Christmas tree

- HAVE A SLEEPOVER UNDER A
  CHRISTMAS TREE
- MAKE A CARD FOR SOMEONE
- WRAP CHRISTMAS PRESENTS
- LISTEN TO MY OLD CHRISTMAS
  RECORDS
- COOK A CHRISTMAS MEAL
- TELL A FRIEND ABOUT THIS LIST
  AND LET THEM HELP YOU!

After I finished reading, I felt cold. Mom was right; normally, I *love* making lists. I love the feeling I get when I cross off an item. *Check, check, double check!* But this list was different. I didn't want to disappoint Mom—but even so, I still didn't want to celebrate Christmas. Right after she'd died, I guess I sort of made a pact with myself: The world might still be spinning, but that didn't mean I had to enjoy it.

And I definitely didn't want to enjoy it this year. Not in Melanie's house, surrounded by Melanie's things. This year may not be as bad as last year—Black Christmas—but it still wasn't great. It was only slightly better. Gray Christmas, I guess.

I wasn't sure I could finish everything on the list,

anyway, even if I wanted to. A lot of the items were doable. Others, like sledding and making a snow angel, I didn't see how I could get those done, not without asking Dad to take me somewhere where it actually snows, and during the Christmas season he works nearly every day. The very first one, roast marshmallows in the fire pit, would be really hard, too. My old house had a fire pit in the backyard, and we used it all the time. But the new house didn't have one.

I bet Mom never imagined that by the time I opened her letter I'd be living in a different house with Dad and his new wife.

I needed to talk to someone, but technically I was still grounded for one more day. Last month Izzy, Sophia, Daisy, and I got into a ton of trouble. We were trying to help Izzy earn charms for her bracelet for a home study course called Mrs. Whippie's Earn Your Charm School and things had gone a little haywire after Izzy decided she'd earn her charm to "beautify" something by anonymously painting a wall in our middle school orange. Everyone had gotten really upset over it. Mrs. Whippie turned out to be Izzy's great aunt Mildred, but we didn't find that out until after we'd all been grounded for the month—except for last weekend, when Izzy's parents took us hot-air-ballooning to earn the last charm Aunt

Mildred had given us. They took us a little early because that was the only Saturday everyone could go. I wasn't supposed to go anywhere without Dad and Melanie, and since they'd taken away my cell phone, I couldn't talk to anyone after school, either.

Or so they thought.

I went into my closet and shut the door. Joey was right; it was a pretty good size. I wedged myself between some boxes of clothes and pulled my walkie-talkie from my backpack. Izzy has a matching walkie-talkie. We used to call each other on them when we were younger, and we started using them again a couple months ago since Izzy isn't allowed to have a cell phone.

"Wordnerd to Stargazer, do you copy?" I said, using our code names. I waited for a few minutes, but when Izzy didn't respond, I put the walkie aside—I'd call her again in a few minutes—and started unpacking all my books and stacking them in my bookcase. Once I'd filled it up, I went back into my closet and tried the walkie again. "Wordnerd to Stargazer, do you copy?"

After a few minutes, Izzy's voice came through with a burst of static. "I copy, Wordnerd. Report your position."

"I'm . . . I'm in enemy territory," I said, because I wasn't ready to call it *home* yet.

Izzy's voice softened. "How's the house?"

"Stupid. It's all white and sterile, and it smells like toilet cleaner. You'd hate it. And she said we can't paint the walls." No need to clarify who "she" was.

Even through the static, I could hear Izzy scowling. "Someone needs to tell the Hammer your house isn't her classroom. Other people should get a say."

Izzy and I had been secretly talking on our walkie-talkies all month, and hearing her voice through the static always makes me feel better. We used to be best friends, but after Mom got sick the idea of leaving the house— leaving Mom—made me nervous. I thought nothing bad could happen to her if I was there. I didn't want to pretend to be a spy or jump in puddles or hang out in Izzy's tree house, so when Izzy would come and knock on my front door, I would ask Dad to tell her I couldn't play. Pretty soon after that, we stopped hanging out.

But I was really glad we were friends again; talking to Izzy every night was the only good part of the last month.

"Anyway," I said. "How are things at your house?"

"Terrible. Mom is on my case about my new skirt. She says it makes me look like a vagrant—whatever *that* means—and she's threatening to take it away. *And* she's still upset over my progress report—she told me if I don't start getting all my homework done, she's going to camp out in my room and watch me do it . . ."

Okay, so this is the one thing I don't like about our daily calls: Izzy always finds time to complain about her mom. I know Mrs. Malone can be tough to live with, but still, sometimes I get tired of hearing about it. When Izzy's going on and on, sometimes I just want to take her by the shoulders and yell, "Don't you know how lucky you are? *Who cares* if your mom is nagging you about your homework? That's normal. Here's a news flash for you: Nobody ever died from doing homework. It will not actually kill you. You will not actually die."

I would never say anything like that, though, no matter how much I want to sometimes. I don't want Izzy to get mad at me, not when we've just become friends again. Mostly, I just try to listen. Mom used to say that everyone needs someone to listen to them, and I know that—lucky or not—a lot of times Izzy doesn't get that from her mom.

". . . and *then* she said she doesn't care if today's the last day of our grounding," Izzy was saying, "and that if I don't stop mouthing off, she'll ground me again."

"That sounds tough," I said. "But I wanted to tell you something. While I was cleaning my old room today I found—"

Suddenly, I heard the door to my room open, followed by a tentative voice saying, "Violet?" It was Melanie.

I froze. I didn't want her to find me hiding in the closet, and I definitely didn't want her to find out I'd been talking to Izzy on the walkie, but also . . . she didn't knock. I'd closed the door after Joey left, and she just walked right in.

"Violet, are you in here?" she called again. Quickly, I shut off the walkie.

I kept quiet, and I was glad I did, because I heard soft footsteps and small thuds, like maybe she was looking through one of my boxes, followed by a long silence. I held my breath and hoped she wouldn't think to open the closet door.

"What are you doing?" That was Dad. It sounded like he'd stopped in the doorway.

"Looking for Violet—and Joey. I can't find either of them. Have you seen them?"

"They're around here somewhere. Where do you want this box?"

"That one goes in Olivia's room. . . ." Their voices faded, and when I was sure they weren't coming back, I turned the walkie-talkie on.

"Violet? Violet, are you there?" Izzy sounded irritated.

"Sorry—Melanie barged into my room. I think she

was spying on me. I really hate her. I can't believe I'm stuck living with her." I looked down at my mother's envelope, and suddenly, I didn't feel like telling Izzy about it anymore. Listening to Melanie poke around my room made the moment seem tainted somehow.

"It stinks," Izzy agreed. "Once we're off grounding, we'll have to hang out at my house. Oh, and Aunt Mildred told me she wants you, Daisy, Sophia, and me to meet her at the Kaleidoscope Café before the tree-lighting tomorrow night. She says, since we'll be off grounding, she has a task and a charm for us."

I thought once we'd discovered Aunt Mildred was Mrs. Whippie, that would be it for earning charms. But instead, we'd all decided to form a club—the Charm Girls Club. I couldn't wait to start adding charms to my bracelet, because to me, each charm represented a moment of fun and good times with Izzy, Daisy, and Sophia, and I wanted to collect more.

"Do you know what she has planned?" I asked.

"No idea," Izzy answered. "I snuck into her room to see if I could find any charms she might have bought, but she caught me midsnoop. I'm not allowed in her room anymore."

I laughed and said, "I guess we'll have to wait and see."

We both said good-bye, and I clicked off the walkie-talkie and stepped out of my closet.

Olivia was standing in my room, glaring at me like I was something disgusting she'd found on the bottom of her shoe.

Seriously, doesn't *anyone* around here have any sense of privacy?

"You're not supposed to be on your cell phone," she said, crossing her arms.

"I wasn't. And *you're* not supposed to be snooping in my room. Or spying on me."

"Um, hello? I've got better things to do than spy on you."

"Doesn't look like it to me," I said.

Olivia put her hands on her hips. "Here's a little PSA from me to you: Your closet is *right next* to my bedroom. I can hear everything you're saying."

Oops. I thought back to all the stuff I'd said about Melanie. "I'll remember that. But feel free not to spy on my conversations."

"I wasn't spying," she repeated. "But *you* could stop being such a jerk all the time."

"How am I being jerk? I've barely said anything to anyone today."

"You barely say anything to anyone, *ever*. That's the problem. Everyone knows you're unhappy. It's casting a pall over the entire house."

That's actually one thing I like about Olivia: She uses interesting words. After she stomped out of my room, I looked up "pall" in my dictionary. It means "anything that covers, shrouds, or overspreads, especially with darkness and gloom." It could also mean, "to have a wearying or tiresome effect, or to become distasteful and unpleasant."

That's me all right. Tiresome and distasteful, just because I'm not jumping for joy over Dad's new family— even though I've gone out of my way to keep my mouth shut.

I highlighted "pall" in neon pink in my dictionary. I like to mark the words I look up in different colors. It's my goal one day to look up every single word, so that when you open it, the whole dictionary looks like a rainbow on the inside.

"Dinner's ready!" Melanie called.

I closed my dictionary, but I didn't leave my room right away. I wanted to put off the moment when I sat down to dinner. It felt like when I did, that would be the real start of our brand-new family, and I wasn't ready for that yet.

Melanie had made chicken tacos, and everyone was

at the counter loading up their plates when I finally came into the kitchen. Dad was standing next to Olivia, laughing as she told him about something that had happened in her math class last week. If you didn't know better, you'd think *she* was his daughter.

"Oh shoot!" Dad said, after he dropped a glob of shredded chicken onto the counter. "Does anyone have a napkin?"

"I'll get it," Olivia and I both said, but she was faster.

"Thanks, Olivia, you're so helpful," Dad said.

She *was* helpful. Pouring him a glass of water. Pulling out his chair for him. Was she seriously trying to replace me? I wondered if that's how Melanie and Olivia saw themselves: Dad's Replacement Family—for the one that had broken apart. The only problem was, I was still around and they couldn't ship me off to the Goodwill with all the rest of Dad's things they hadn't wanted to keep.

"Hey, Champ," Dad said, "let's get a move on, okay?"

"Okay." I turned away and grabbed a plate. Since I'm a vegetarian, I filled my taco shell with beans, cheese, and veggies. When I turned to join everyone, my mouth got a little dry, because they were all sitting around the table, looking like the perfect family of four. But I didn't see a fifth chair.

"Ahem." I cleared my throat.

"Violet, come join us," Melanie said, glancing up briefly. She seemed distracted. They all did. The chicken was runny and dripping out of the taco shells and all over everyone's plate.

I stood there another moment, but no one noticed there wasn't anywhere for me to sit. "I can't," I said finally.

"What?" Dad asked, wiping his hands with a napkin.

"I can't join you. There's no fifth chair."

Dad and Melanie looked up and stared at each other. They wore the surprised, frustrated expression adults get when they realize they've forgotten something important.

Melanie's brow furrowed. "I thought you were going to buy another chair last night?" she said to Dad.

"I couldn't find a matching one," Dad said, sighing. "I'm so sorry, Champ—I completely forgot about it today." He looked back at Melanie. "I think we should just buy a new dining set, altogether."

"But this was my grandmother's table," Melanie said. "It's an antique."

"Exactly. Which is why we won't be able to find a matching chair."

While they talked, Olivia shot me an annoyed glance. "What?" I mouthed at her. How was any of this *my* fault?

Dad and Mom's table-and-chair set had six chairs—but of course, the Hammer didn't like it, so off it went to the Goodwill. Meanwhile, my plate of tacos was starting to feel heavy.

"We can use one of the folding chairs for the time being," Melanie said. "I'm sure we'll find a match soon. This table has been in my family for ages."

"It hasn't been in *my* family," Dad said sharply.

Everyone was silent after that. Dad and Melanie stared at each other. Joey looked like he was going to start crying. Suddenly, I was seized with a pang in my stomach so strong I thought I'd split in two—it was the Terrible Beautiful Ache, no doubt about it.

I didn't want to be here, surrounded by Melanie's things and Melanie's family. I wanted *my* things. *My* family. I wanted to be somewhere I didn't have to hold my tongue or worry about tracking mud into the house.

I wanted Mom.

Melanie started to get up. "Violet, I'm so sorry. You can have my—"

I set my plate on the counter. "I'm fine," I said as I turned to head back to my room. "The tacos don't look that great, anyway."

CHAPTER 5

ONE FOOT IN FRONT OF THE OTHER

Mom used to say, when you don't know where you're going, just keep putting one foot in front of the other, and eventually, you'll get where you need to be. I always thought it was a strange saying—after all, if you don't know where you're going, how will you know when you've reached wherever it is you need to be?

I thought about that as Dad, Melanie, Joey, Olivia, and I all grabbed our coats and headed out the door and into the night. We were walking to the tree-lighting, which was being held in Dandelion Square. None of us were used to a crowded house, and for the last day and a half, we'd all been tiptoeing around one another, being real polite and saying "please" and "thank you" a lot. It felt like we were all walking on glass: You press just a tiny bit too hard, and everything could shatter and break apart.

Joey raced ahead looking for houses already decorated with Christmas lights—Melanie and Olivia following along behind him—and Dad dropped back to talk to me.

"Here," he said, handing me my cell phone. "You are officially off grounding—but no texting until we actually get there tonight."

"Oh, thank you!" I said, hugging it to myself like it was a long-lost friend.

Dad laughed. "You were a good sport about not having it."

"Uh, yeah," I said. I felt slightly guilty about my nightly chats with Izzy. Even though Dad never actually said I couldn't use the walkie-talkie, I was pretty sure, if I'd asked him, he'd have said that it violated the spirit of the law of my grounding, if not the letter.

We walked in silence, until Dad said, "Did you open it?"

I made my eyes go real wide, and said, "Open what?"

He sighed. "Violet, come on."

I felt at my jacket pocket, where I'd stashed Mom's letter. I probably had it memorized by now. Dad had pretty much left me alone for the last day, and I'd been glad for a little space.

"Yeah, I opened it," I said.

"And?"

"And . . . she left me a list."

"A list?" Dad frowned. "What kind of a list?"

"Dad . . . do we have to talk about this now?"

"I guess not . . . not if you don't want to. I know you're getting older, Champ. I know sometimes you'd rather talk to someone else other than me—a woman, I guess. Maybe sometime Melanie could . . ."

I looked over at him. "Seriously? You want me to talk to *Melanie* about Mom's letter?"

Dad put his arm around me. "As long as you talk to someone, Champ. I worry about you, you know."

"Well, you don't have to," I said. "Because I'm fine."

Just then, Joey doubled back and slipped his hand into mine. "I'm getting tired of walking," he complained.

"Me too," I answered. "But we're not that far away. Just keep putting one foot in front of the other, and eventually, we'll get there."

CHAPTER

6

BACK IN
BUSINESS!

Dandelion Square is a large village green in the middle of downtown Dandelion Hollow, complete with park benches, a fountain, a gazebo, and a small playground. When we arrived, the square was crowded and already decorated for Christmas. White twinkle lights were strung between the old-fashioned lampposts, each of which was adorned with a large green wreath. More lights framed the windows of the shops lining the square, and the air smelled cold and crisp.

"Violet, where are you going?" Melanie asked, after I turned to head for the Kaleidoscope Café.

"To find my friends," I said. "We're supposed to meet up tonight."

"No, we're—" Melanie began, just as Dad said, "Have fun, Champ."

The Kaleidoscope Café is one of my favorite places in Dandelion Hollow. The menu is always changing, and Ms. Zubov, the owner, usually gives me free slices of pie.

Inside, the café smelled like cinnamon and sugar, and jazzy Christmas carols were playing on the old jukebox. Aunt Mildred, Izzy, and Daisy were already there, sitting at a booth in the back. Aunt Mildred had four small boxes wrapped in pale pink wrapping paper on the table in front of her.

"Hey," I said, sliding into the booth next to Daisy, who was scribbling away in a small notebook. "What are you writing?"

"An article for the *Grapevine* about tonight," she said. Her short blond hair bobbed as she wrote even faster. "I'm almost finished."

I frowned. "I thought Olivia was writing that article?" Olivia was the sixth-grade editor of the *Grapevine*, the school newspaper—a position that Daisy had wanted.

"It wasn't assigned to me. I was just going to surprise everyone with it tomorrow. But if Olivia's already writing about it . . ." She scowled and flipped her notebook closed.

Then she looked at me, and said, "How was your weekend with the Hammer?"

I didn't like the look in her eyes—sort of a mixture of pity and hesitation, like she didn't exactly know what to say. It was a look I'd seen a lot the last couple years, and I was sick of it. So I just shrugged, and said, "It was fine."

Sophia came bursting into the café, her face flushed from the cold. "Sorry I'm late," she said, sliding into the booth.

"How was your Thanksgiving?" I asked her.

"Busy," she answered, yawning as she tucked a strand of long brown hair behind her ear. "The shop's been packed all weekend." Sophia's mother, Mrs. Ramos, owns Charming Trinkets, the jewelry shop just around the corner, where Aunt Mildred buys our charms. A lot of times Sophia helps her mom out by working at the store or by watching her younger twin brothers.

Izzy clapped her hands together. "Finally, we're all here—the charm girls are back in business!" She reached for a box, but Aunt Mildred swept it out of her way.

"You're back in business, provided you don't get in trouble earning these charms," she said. "I need a promise from all of you that you'll stay out of trouble this time."

"I promise," Sophia said quickly.

"Me too," I said.

"Define 'trouble,'" Izzy said, and Daisy nodded seriously.

"Izzy," Aunt Mildred warned.

"Just kidding!" Izzy said. "I promise."

"Yeah, me too," Daisy said, although both she and Izzy looked a little reluctant.

"Okay, now that that's settled." Aunt Mildred passed out the boxes.

We ripped them open. Inside were two charms. The first was a tiny clock charm and the second, a small candy cane. The clock charm was golden and vintage-looking with hour hands that actually moved. The candy-cane charm was red and white and looked so real I could swear I smelled peppermint.

Once we finished examining the charms, we all looked up expectantly at Aunt Mildred.

"How do we earn these?" Sophia asked.

"I've been talking with the Caulfields," Aunt Mildred said. "Turns out, they need a little extra help on the weekends with their Christmas-tree lot. So I've volunteered you four for this Saturday—you're going to give them the gift of your time, hence the clock charm."

"Awesome!" Sophia said. "I've always wanted to work on a tree lot!"

"Volunteer?" Daisy said, wrinkling her nose. "Are you

kidding? I thought we were going to be doing something *fun*—like hot-air-ballooning last weekend. You always make us do—"

"I don't always make you do *anything*, Daisy Caulfield," Aunt Mildred said, looking perturbed. "You're free to give back the charms, if you wish—but for your information, your grandma told me you were going to be working on the farm this month, no matter what, so you might want to pipe down."

Daisy and her mom had moved back to Dandelion Hollow last summer and were living on her grandparents' farm, and I knew she got pretty sick of farm work.

"What about the candy-cane charm?" I asked.

"The rotary club purchased a ton of candy canes to give away tonight," Aunt Mildred said. "They need people to pass them out."

"What, you mean *now*?" Izzy said.

"No, I mean two hours from now, after everyone's gone home," Aunt Mildred said. "Yes, I mean *now*." She took a sip of coffee. "Don't look so disappointed," she said to Daisy. "Next time, I promise not to make you do something for the common good."

"Are you passing out candy canes with us?" Sophia asked.

Aunt Mildred shook her head. "I'm helping Scooter. He's playing Santa tonight, and he needs an assistant."

"Is Scooter your boyfriend now?" Daisy asked.

It was something the four of us had been wondering all month. Scooter McGee owns the Dusty Shelf—a used bookstore a few shops away from the café—and he and Aunt Mildred had a lunch date at Pumpkin Palooza, Dandelion Hollow's annual fall festival, last month, and they'd been spending a lot of time together ever since. Izzy told me that Scooter had had a crush on Aunt Mildred back when they were in high school together, and now, forty years later, he still liked her.

Forty years—I couldn't even imagine liking the same boy for forty *days*.

"I am entirely too old to be having boyfriends." Aunt Mildred sniffed.

"If you don't like the word 'boyfriend,'" Izzy said, "we could always go with 'beau' or 'gentleman caller' or 'hot—'"

"Izzy," Aunt Mildred said in a warning voice, "you're about to get on my last nerve."

"You mean you've got more than one?" Izzy teased.

Everyone laughed; then we gathered our charms and left the café to go find the rotary club.

We don't get snow in Dandelion Hollow—in our part of northern California, we're lucky if we get rain—so instead of snowflakes, machines were spraying multicolored bubbles into the air, making it hard to see. Tyler Jones and a couple other boys from school were easily visible, though; they had gotten ahold of some jingle bells and were running around and ringing them in people's ears. Over at the gazebo, there was a line of people waiting to get a picture taken with Santa. Just beyond stood a large spruce tree, unlit, but already laden with Christmas ornaments.

"Laden"—it means, "heavily loaded or weighed down." That's how I felt as the four of us pushed through the crowd. Like I carried a hundred-pound weight on my chest as I watched all the happy families laughing and smiling at one another.

"Isn't this awesome?" Sophia said excitedly.

"Amazing," I lied.

Sophia turned to me, looking worried. "Are you sure? You look like something's wrong?"

I thought about telling her about Mom's letter or about the Terrible Beautiful Ache that was pressing on me or how this was the first tree-lighting I'd been to since Mom died because Dad and I skipped it last year. But everyone looked so happy, and I didn't want to spoil things.

Trust me, you mention a dead parent and people—even your closest friends—get real uncomfortable, real fast.

"It's nothing," I said. "I'm fine."

We found the president of the rotary club, who gave us each a box of candy canes and told us to fan out into the square. I passed mine out one by one, watching all the happy families as shiny soap bubbles from the "snow" machine danced across the air. I wished there was real snow tonight. Mom and Dad used to take me up to Lake Tahoe every winter to go sledding, but the first thing when we arrived, Mom and I would flop onto our backs and make snow angels. Then we'd make a big deal of showing them to Dad.

"Snow angels from my two angels," Dad would say every year.

It was our tradition, and it was corny and mushy and totally not cool—but I loved it, anyway.

I was down to my last two candy canes when I heard a loud voice behind me say, "No, it's *not* okay. You should have told me."

I turned around and saw Austin Jackson, one of my classmates, standing next to his parents. "Told you what?" I asked.

"None of your business!" he snapped. "I wasn't talking to *you*."

"Austin!" Mr. Jackson said. "You're being rude."

"*I'm* being rude?" Austin said, whirling back around to face his dad. "You're being rude. You could've told me—"

"Austin!" Mrs. Jackson gave him a stern look. "Not *here*."

"Fine, whatever," Austin said, and stalked away.

"I'm sorry, Violet," Mrs. Jackson said as we watched Austin push into the crowd. "I don't know what's come over him tonight."

"It's fine," I said, handing Mr. and Mrs. Jackson each a candy cane. Sophia appeared next to me, her box empty.

"What was that about?" she asked, glancing over at the Jacksons once we'd walked away from them.

"No idea," I said. "Typical boy weirdness."

Except Austin wasn't just any boy. He was Izzy's next-door neighbor, and she used to have a crush on him. I could understand why she'd liked him. He was cute and usually pretty nice—when he wasn't acting like a total tool.

We ran into Izzy and Daisy; they'd also just finished passing out their candy canes. Together, the four of us removed our charm bracelets and began hooking our candy-cane charms onto the golden chains.

"We have earned our charm," Izzy said, raising her voice

over all the commotion in the square. I guess to someone else, it could sound a little corny, but it made me feel warm inside, to be staring at Izzy, Daisy, and Sophia and see them smiling back at me, wearing their identical bracelets.

It made the night feel a little bit easier.

Just then Tyler Jones came running up to Izzy and rang a pair of jingle bells right next to her ear. "Merry Christmas, Toad Girl!" he yelled. "Toad Girl" is what people sometimes call Izzy; they used to call her that all the time, but it's gotten a lot better in the last month.

"That's *it*," Daisy said as Tyler ran off. "That's the second time tonight he's done that to you, Izzy. I say we get a hold of him and—"

"Forget about it," Izzy said, rubbing her ear. "I'm on a strict diet of forgiveness and good behavior. I am *not* spending another month grounded." She smiled at Daisy and added, "But if *you* want to get some revenge on my behalf, there's really nothing I could do about it, right?"

"Right," Daisy said. "I could use a little Christmas revenge right about now." Daisy ran off in Tyler's direction, Sophia following behind, and Izzy went to find her sister, Carolyn, who was going to be singing Christmas carols with the Dandelion High choir tonight.

I wandered away from everyone, and sat down on a

park bench. I pulled Mom's letter from my jeans pocket. She was right that I loved making lists, and normally, I'd already be reaching for my pen and checking off "Attend Dandelion Hollow's Tree-Lighting."

"Well, will you look at that?" said a stuffy voice nearby. "Honestly, the nerve of some people."

I turned; Edith Binchy, a longtime resident of Dandelion Hollow, was sitting with a few ladies from her knitting circle on the park bench behind me. "Over at the gazebo," she added.

I glanced over. Joey was sitting on Santa's—Scooter's—lap while Olivia stood just to his side. The photographer snapped a picture, and then Scooter beckoned to Dad and Melanie to join them. Dad and Melanie glanced at each other and shrugged, then joined in for another picture while Aunt Mildred held Melanie's purse. I felt another Terrible Beautiful Ache go through me, like someone was plucking an out-of-tune violin.

"I can't believe he married that woman. I mean, what was Mitch *thinking*?"

I tried not to listen, since they were talking about Dad and Melanie. Gossip is one of Dandelion Hollow's favorite pastimes, and Edith Binchy's knitting circle, the Knattering Knitters, was famous for being huge gossipers. Izzy's grandma Bertie was a part of it, but Edith Binchy was probably the worst of the lot.

I didn't like that they were gossiping about Dad and Melanie, but in a weird way, I understood it. Melanie had lived in Dandelion Hollow for only a few years, but Mom had grown up here. She had been the town's favorite piano teacher. Addison Binchy, Edith's granddaughter, had actually been one of Mom's students.

"Candy cane?" I said, waving my box in the Knatters' general direction, even though it was empty. A few of the ladies had enough sense to at least pretend to look ashamed that I'd caught them gossiping about Dad.

"Violet, sweetheart, how *are* you?" Edith asked, fake concern flashing in her eyes.

"Couldn't be better," I said, smiling wide. When someone you love dies, at first people understand why you're sad. But after a certain amount of time has passed, they expect you to be happy again. Besides, I was pretty sure whatever I said would be repeated all over town.

"Buzz off, Edith," Aunt Mildred said, coming up beside me. "And take your hive of busybodies with you. Go get your daily dirt somewhere else."

"Well." Edith sniffed. "Bertie told us you were difficult." Izzy's grandma Bertie is Aunt Mildred's twin sister, and the two of them fight like teenagers.

"I'll bet she did. Say, if you want some gossip, you wanna know what I heard about that no-good son of yours?"

Edith gave a shocked exclamation, then herded the Knatterers away.

"Good riddance," Aunt Mildred said, sitting down next to me. "I went to high school with Edith Binchy—what an impossible woman."

A loud *thump* sounded on the village green; Mayor Franklin tapped on the microphone that was set up next to the Christmas tree. "Attention, everyone! If you could all gather round!"

Aunt Mildred scowled and muttered a couple words under her breath. Last month Izzy's mom had run against Mrs. Franklin in the mayoral race. Mrs. Malone had lost pretty badly, and Izzy's family was still mad about it.

Aunt Mildred and I stood up and joined the crowd in front of the tree. I found Dad, Melanie, Joey, and Olivia, and stood behind them. Dad turned and caught sight of me and said, "*There* you are. We were looking all over for you."

It didn't look like it when you were taking a family picture with Santa, I wanted to say, but like usual, I kept quiet.

"Welcome to Dandelion Hollow's annual tree-lighting ceremony!"

I didn't hear anything else Mayor Franklin said, or the Dandelion High choir when they started singing carols, because I was watching Dad. His hand was on Melanie's back and he kept laughing as she whispered in his ear.

I remembered when Dad used to look at Mom like that. Like they were the only two people in the world. Mom always used to say that Dad was "the One" for her. But now that Dad and Melanie were married, did that mean that Melanie was "the One" for Dad?

As soon as the choir finished singing, the tree lit up, sparkling and shining, and a cheer went up from the crowd.

"It's beautiful, isn't it?" Melanie said.

"It sure is," Dad agreed, but he wasn't looking at the tree. He was still looking at Melanie. Dad linked his arm with hers, and turned to me. "Don't you think so, Champ?"

"Sure," I said. "It looks great."

Then I picked a candy cane up off the ground. It was uneaten and still wrapped in cellophane. Someone had tossed the whole thing away, like it was completely worthless.

CHAPTER 7

COOKIES AND SODA

Dad works long hours at Barnaby's Antiques—the shop he owns over on Dandelion Square. Most days he's already at work before I wake up in the morning, and he doesn't get home until dinnertime, when we usually order takeout. I was pretty used to having quiet mornings to myself, so it was a little strange Monday when I walked into the kitchen and found Melanie, Olivia, and Joey there, eating breakfast. The morning news was on in the background, Joey was banging on his cereal bowl, and Olivia was talking about a school-newspaper meeting she had later today.

"Good morning, Violet," Melanie said.

"Morning," I mumbled. I ignored the plate of bacon she offered me and headed for the fridge, wishing the three of them didn't have to be so loud.

"Oreos and soda aren't a healthy breakfast," Melanie announced in a tight voice when I joined them at the table.

"Oh," I said when she pushed the plate of bacon toward me. "Thanks . . . but I don't eat meat."

Olivia rolled her eyes, but Melanie smacked her forehead. "You're a vegetarian, I forgot."

I didn't see how she kept forgetting. Didn't want to remember, was probably more like it, and I figured she hoped it was a phase I'd snap out of pretty soon.

Except it wasn't a phase. After Mom got sick, Dad went out and bought a ton of books on cancer and nutrition. He stayed up late every night reading them, then announced one day that we were all becoming vegetarians and were eating only organic produce. By the frantic look in his eyes, I knew not to argue.

The night after Mom died, he came home with takeout hamburgers and ate them defiantly, muttering a bunch of bad words the whole time. I looked at mine and thought I was going to be sick. I threw it away later that night, when all the lights in the house were turned off and I could hear muffled sobs coming from Dad's room.

"I'll make you some toast," Melanie said.

"Thank you, that's really nice," I forced myself to say in a polite voice. "But I'm fine, really. It's no big deal."

Olivia glared at me. "Whatever, Violet—no one has time for your theatrics today."

"Theatrics"—it means, "exaggerated mannerisms, actions, or words." Basically, being overly dramatic, and I didn't see how quietly trying to eat my breakfast qualified as being dramatic. *They* were the ones causing a racket this morning and freaking out over my breakfast choices.

"You never let *us* eat cookies in the morning," Joey said to Melanie furiously. "*I* want an Oreo, too."

Melanie chewed on her cheek. "Violet . . . in my house, we don't have cookies and soda for breakfast."

In *her* house? Another ache went through me.

"I have cookies and soda for breakfast all the time and Dad doesn't care," I said. Well, actually, Dad probably had no clue what I ate for breakfast, but Melanie didn't need to know that. Besides, why did I have to be the one who changed? The three of them had already taken over the house—why couldn't I keep one tiny piece of the life Dad and I used to have, even if it was just a stupid plate of Oreos?

"Violet." Melanie sighed. "I'm just trying to give everyone a good, healthy home."

I had a good home—you're the reason I had to move out of it, I said only to myself. To Melanie, I said, "Got it. No more cookies and soda for breakfast."

I left the kitchen, grabbed my coat and backpack, and headed for school, determined to get as far away from Melanie and *her* house as fast as I could.

8

Bursting with Fruit Flavors

When something bad happens to you, people assume that you should Talk About It. It's healthy, they say. It's good for you. And if you *don't want* to Talk About It, well then, something must be wrong with you, and it needs to be fixed. *You* need to be fixed.

After Mom passed away, I didn't want to talk about it. Talking about it can't change it. One minute you're normal, the next you're the Girl with a Dead Mother. And no amount of talking or crying or pleading can change that, so what's the point?

Dad didn't want to talk about it, either, but he figured I ought to, so he made me see the guidance counselor at my old elementary school: Mrs. Mudge, who was like a hundred years old, and seemed to take it personally when I didn't talk to her, either.

I thought I was done with those visits once middle school started, but the second week of school, I got a note to go to the office, where I met my new guidance counselor, Coco Martin. She likes to pretend to be all tough, but I know she really likes me, and that feels nice, even if I spend most of my time during our sessions *not* answering her questions.

Whenever I visit, Coco ignores the chairs in front of her desk and has us sit in two squashy beanbags in the corner of her office. They're really comfy and I like them, but it's also a reminder that I'm not here because I've gotten in trouble. I'm here because something terrible has happened, and she wants to see how I'm doing.

"So," Coco said after we settled in. "Let's talk."

"Talk?" I feigned surprise. "About what?"

Coco didn't roll her eyes at me, but I could tell she wanted to. "School. Life. Your new stepmother."

"Now why would I want to talk about things like that?" I said.

"Some people think it's normal in a situation like this," she said. "They call it therapy."

"Oh yeah? Well, some people think it's normal to eat fish eggs. They call it sushi." I leaned back in my chair. "What else you got?"

Coco pretended to think about it. "New house?"

"Yes," I agreed. "New houses exist."

Now Coco actually did roll her eyes. "Don't try to outsmart-aleck me, Violet. I'm a professional. You've got to give me something to work with, okay? Besides, I've got Trent Walker sitting in the hall, and I'd be happy to keep him waiting all day if I have to." She settled deeper into her beanbag and stretched. "Man, these are *really* comfortable, don't you think?"

I sighed. "All right, *fine*. It's only been a couple days, but so far Melanie has managed to get rid of a bunch of our stuff, she's telling me what I can and cannot eat for breakfast, and I'm pretty sure she's not going to let me paint my bedroom walls. There. Are you happy now?"

"Ecstatic," Coco replied. "I'm bursting with fruit flavors."

"Bursting with fruit flavors" is one of Coco's favorite phrases. I'm not exactly sure what it means. But I think it might mean that she's happy on the inside, or that right now life feels sweet, and not very sour.

"But seriously," Coco continued. "I'm worried about

you. You seemed a lot happier last month. You made some great friends. You have that bracelet club that you and Izzy are starting—she told me all about it the last time she got sent here."

"Why did Izzy get sent here?" I asked, curious.

"Can't tell you that—but let's just say that girl needs to learn there's a time and a place to tell someone off. Anyway, my point is, you seemed happier last month. I know this past week can't have been easy. Are you sure you don't want to tell me a little more about what's going on with you?"

I shrugged again. I *was* having a great time last month helping Izzy earn her charms. But that was before Dad got engaged to Melanie, before everyone started talking about the holidays, and I realized that Black Christmas wasn't just a one-time thing. Christmas without Mom is the new normal.

"What about the letter?" she continued.

I paused. "What?"

Seriously? Can't I have just a little bit of privacy? I knew Dad and Coco chatted sometimes, but this was ridiculous.

I guess my irritation showed, because Coco said, "Your dad called this morning and left me a voice mail that you received a special letter. He's worried about you. He said you barely said two words over the weekend. He said you're separating yourself from everyone else in the house."

I stared over Coco's shoulder at the wall behind her. She likes to plaster her office with posters with different sayings on them. The one directly behind her read, "Be a rainbow in someone else's cloud." I figured Dad must have called Coco because he and Melanie thought I was the opposite of that: I was the gray cloud hanging over their shiny new-family rainbow. And in a rainbow, there's just no room for gray.

"Who was it from?" Coco asked.

"My mom," I answered.

Coco looked surprised. "Your mom? I don't understand."

"She wrote it before, well, you know." I hesitated, but then removed the letter from my backpack and gave it to her. While she read, her eyes became glassy. "This is wondrous," she said.

"Wondrous?" I repeated.

Coco nodded and handed it back to me. "Look it up later in that dictionary you're so proud of. I think 'wondrous' is the perfect word to describe it. . . . Actually, that gives me an idea. I've got an assignment for you. I want *you* to write a letter."

"A letter to you?" I said.

"To anyone. It doesn't matter who—you don't even have to send it. I'm worried that you're keeping a lot of your feelings pent up. If you can't talk about how you're feeling, I'd like you to write about it."

I didn't see how writing a letter would make anything better. But there were so many things I had never told anyone, because I didn't think they'd understand. Maybe it would be nice just to put it on paper—maybe even write it in my purple journal, where no one would ever see it.

I left not too long after that. Maybe I wasn't bursting with fruit flavors. But I wasn't feeling sour, either.

9

PARTNERS

When your stepmother is the meanest teacher in the world, school is just a bundle of good times. People had been talking about Dad and Melanie all month, and this morning was no different after I left Coco's office and made my way to second period.

"Hey—your new mommy gave me an F on my test," a guy from my math class called, and the group of boys he was hanging out with sniggered.

"She's not my mother," I shot back. "And maybe you got an F because you're a moron."

"Hey, Hammerhead, what's up?" Tyler Jones said as I passed him and Austin. "Hey! Didn't you hear me?

Hammerhead? Get it? Don't you think I'm funny?"

"Hysterical," I called, flipping around and walking backward so I could stare at him. "Your ingenuity amazes me."

"Ange-*what*? Listen Nerd Brain—"

"Tyler!" Austin slammed his locker. "Shut up!"

Austin ran to catch up with me. "Sorry about that." Austin and I both have history with Miss Mallery for second period, so we continued down the hall together.

"Don't worry about it," I said. "It's not your fault Tyler has the personality of a dirty toenail."

Austin grinned, and said, "Listen—about the tree-lighting last night. i'm sorry I was kind of a jerk."

I raised my eyebrows. "*Kind* of a jerk?"

"All right, a huge jerk."

"A ginormous jerk," I agreed.

"Wait—" He grabbed my arm before I could step inside Miss Mallery's classroom. "There's this cooking school in New York that my mom has always dreamed of going to. I guess she applied, and got in. She's flying to New York next week to check it out. And if she likes it, she'll come back for Christmas, but then leave again next month. Her program would run from January through September."

"So she'd be living in New York all that time?" I asked as students streamed past us into the classroom.

Austin nodded. "I guess it's her dream or something. She and Dad have been talking about it for a while—but they didn't tell me until right before we left for the tree-lighting. That's why I was mad. I didn't mean to be a jerk, I swear. I just thought they could have told me earlier, you know? Instead of just springing it on me. But she said, what if this is her big opportunity, her shot to pursue her dream and she never gets another one like it?"

"What if?" I murmured. I'd repeated those two words a lot the last couple years.

"I know she'd only be gone less than a year," Austin continued. "It's not the end of the world. It's not like she's dying—" Austin's eyes widened with horror as he realized what he'd just said, and who he'd said it to. "Violet, I'm so sorry. I'm such a nerd."

"You're a total nerd," I agreed. "But it's okay. . . . Seriously, it's fine," I added when he tried to apologize again.

At least Austin understood there was a difference between missing his mom because she was maybe going away to cooking school for a year and me missing my mom because she had passed away. Once, a few days after Mom's funeral, Stella Franklin told me she knew how I felt because her dog had just died.

"Anyways," Austin said as the warning bell rang, "I'm sorry."

"Apology accepted," I said.

"Cool." Austin held open the door. "After you."

We slid into seats in the back row and Miss Mallery called the class to attention. "All right, everyone, I have wonderful news!"

Austin glanced at me and rolled his eyes. Miss Mallery was really young and always bounced on the balls of her feet when she was excited—which was pretty much all of the time. She had honey-colored hair, a long face, and warm brown eyes—she sort of reminded me of a golden retriever. Today she was wearing a Santa hat with a bell on the end that jingled each time she bounced up and down.

"Well?" she said, bouncing again. "Don't you want to know what my wonderful news is?"

"No," Austin said quietly, and I had to stifle a laugh.

"*I* want to know what it is," Stella Franklin said.

"Suck-up," Austin muttered.

"Totally," I said, and Austin smiled.

"This month, we're going to be studying the ancient Egyptians!" *Bounce, jingle. Bounce, bounce, jingle.* "And"— she paused dramatically—"you have a project due before winter break starts!"

Groans rose up over the jingling of her Santa hat, but she continued, "You'll be writing an essay on the life and culture of the ancient Egyptians"—*bounce, bounce, jingle, jingle*—"as well as constructing your own Egyptian pyramid! It will be a lot of work. But I know you can do it!" She ended her speech by throwing her hands in the air, like she was a cheerleader with pom-poms.

"Wow," Austin whispered, as we watched her continue to bounce. "There's something *really* wrong with her."

"Seriously," I said.

"Wanna partner up?" he asked.

Austin wasn't someone I'd normally choose for a partner—everyone knows he's practically allergic to homework, and studying in general. But I remembered how it felt when all of a sudden you realize that someone who was always there to take care of you suddenly might not be anymore. Even if it was for a good reason—a once-in-a-lifetime opportunity—I figured it might feel similar. Behind his goofy smile and the way he was bouncing in his seat—trying to mimic Miss Mallery while he waited for me to answer—I wondered if I saw a little bit of a Terrible Beautiful Ache inside of him.

"Sure," I said. "Let's be partners."

10

WHAT IF?

"What If?"

Those two words top my list of Words That Make Me Nervous. I guess for some people "What if?" could be happy words: *What if I won the lottery? What if the cute boy in math class asks me out? What if I never had to do any homework for the rest of my life?* Really, they're just two small words. I guess what matters is how you use them.

For me, when I get all dreary inside, I start thinking things like: *What if Mom had gone to the doctor three months earlier? What if she'd never gotten sick at all? What if I'd watched her every single minute of every single day—could I have detected the exact moment she got cancer? Would it have made a difference?*

I told Dad about my What If? game once, but he said I was wasting my time, and that the past is the past, and you can't ever change it. Then he slammed into his room like he was really mad. But I'm pretty sure he went in there to cry. That's why I don't always tell him stuff, even when he asks. I figure he's got enough dreariness of his own. He doesn't need any of mine.

But all through the rest of my classes, I couldn't help playing the What If? game:

What if Mrs. Jackson likes the cooking school? What if she leaves for ten months and it's just Austin and his dad at home?

What if? What if? What if?

If you're not careful, *What if?* can drive you crazy.

After Mom sat me down and told me she was sick, she and Dad left me alone—so I could get used to the news, I guess. But I didn't want to get used to anything. I was so mad; I wanted to *do* something, but I didn't know what. Finally, I made a list of everything in the house that needed to be cleaned, and then I got started on it, furiously dusting and wiping, until I was too tired to be mad or upset.

As I walked home from school, I remembered there was this vegetable soup Mom used to eat all the time whenever she got a cold. She said it made her feel better, stronger. It stank to high heaven, though, because there was a ton of garlic in it, but I never minded cooking it, because it made me feel like I was being useful. We called it Stinky Soup and it was the first meal I ever made by myself without Mom. Sometimes I still make it, just because it reminds me of her.

So later, after I'd finished my homework, I went to the kitchen and started chopping veggies and peeling garlic. Everything was bubbling away in a stockpot when Melanie came in from the garage.

"What is that god-awful smell?" she said, making a face.

"I'm making soup," I said, giving it a stir.

"Soup?" She checked her watch. "It's a little early for dinner."

"It's not for us," I retorted, deciding right then that it wasn't. My voice sounded sharper than I'd intended, so I tried to soften it. "What were you doing in the garage?"

"Going through some of your dad's stuff. He's got boxes and boxes everywhere. And those old records!" she exclaimed, moving to the sink to wash her hands. "He never gets rid of anything, does he?" She gave me a con-spiratorial smile, like we were in this together. *Can you believe what a packrat your father is?*

I turned back to the stove. I was glad she couldn't see my face. "Those old records were my mother's," I said, stirring the soup slowly. The onions were stinging my eyes, but I didn't wipe them until after Melanie muttered a startled apology and went scurrying back into the garage.

After the soup was done, I poured it into a plastic container, then left to walk it over to the Jacksons. I wanted to get out of the house and I figured *they* might actually appreciate it.

I had to hold the container tightly as I stomped down the street. What right did Melanie have to go through our stuff? The only reason why we still had so many packed boxes was because she obviously preferred her things. Our things—the stuff we'd actually kept—had been relegated to the garage.

At the Jacksons house, I rang the doorbell and waited for someone to answer. "I brought you soup," I blurted after Austin opened the door.

"You brought me soup?" he repeated. Then a wide smile broke out over his face, and he cocked his head. "Heeeeyyy . . . you brought me soup!"

"Yes. No. Sort of," I said, flustered. "It's a recipe my mom liked. She always said it made her feel better. I just made it today and figured . . . maybe you guys would want some?" My face was flaming, and I felt like the biggest dork in the world, because I knew I was making no sense.

Austin's mom wasn't sick; she didn't need a container of soup. Why exactly did I think they'd want some?

But Austin didn't seem to think I was being weird. His grin vanished, along with his cocky demeanor, as he reached out and took the soup.

"Demeanor"—it means "conduct, behavior, or facial appearance."

His facial appearance became tentative as we stood facing each other awkwardly. "Thanks. So . . . do you want to come in or something? I guess we could start planning our Egyptian project."

"Uh, no," I said, backing up a few steps. "I'm good. I've got other homework I need to do." That wasn't exactly true—I always make a Homework List every week and keep ahead of it—but it felt strange, Being Invited Into a Boy's House. Maybe I should've asked a girl to be my partner, because Austin looked cute standing in the doorway in a T-shirt that brought out the blue in his eyes, and I felt even more ridiculous for bringing him soup for no good reason. Who *does* that?

"Okay, well, see you tomorrow," he said.

"Yeah—see you," I said.

The sky was turning dusky as I walked home. I reached into my pocket and pulled out Mom's list. "Cook a Christmas meal," second from the bottom. I don't know that Stinky Soup qualifies as an actual Christmas meal, but I figured the embarrassment I'd suffer if Austin told everyone at school I'd shown up at his doorstep carrying a container of soup made it count. As soon as I got home, I crossed it off the list, and wished I could talk to Mom about how strange it felt, standing on Austin's doorstep while he smiled at me.

Right then, I thought about Coco's assignment to write someone a letter, and suddenly, I knew exactly who to choose.

11

LOVE ALWAYS, VIOLET

Dear Mom,

My guidance counselor told me I should write a letter to someone, and I decided to write to you. Coco says that the best letters are wondrous. I looked that word up, and it means "amazing and delightful," which sounds about right, because it was amazing and delightful to get a letter from you after so many months of wishing I could hear your voice. I don't know if you can see me from heaven or the great beyond or whatever you're supposed to call it, but I like to think that you can. So that means you must know Dad and I just moved in with Melanie, Olivia, and Joey.

I just got your letter this Christmas, and I don't know how to feel about it. I know you want me to find beauty in a new pattern, but there's nothing beautiful about living with the Hammer. I liked the patterns of our old life: how you and Dad would put on one of your old records and dance at night, wood crackling in our fireplace. How you'd play your piano for hours, until I thought if I looked closely enough, I'd see the notes bouncing and bopping across our ceiling. How the lavender bushes would bloom in our backyard every spring, and how you would tie some together with rosemary sprigs for a sweet and spicy bouquet.

You once said, "If you can't say something nice, don't say anything at all." But what happens when everything you're thinking and feeling isn't nice? Do you just stop talking? I wish I'd thought to ask you that back when I had the chance.

It's true that I have a Terrible Beautiful Ache inside of me. Sometimes it presses on me so hard it leaves me speechless. I'm guessing you thought if I did all the things on your list, it would get better. Maybe you're right. Today I made Stinky Soup for Austin Jackson's family, and I decided that should count for making a Christmas meal. It felt good to do something nice for someone else—except I felt weird standing outside Austin's house. For a second, I almost thought he was flirting with me, and I wished you were here so I could talk to you about it.

After I finished homework tonight, I made a Christmas card to mail to Grandma Barnaby, just so I could cross "Make a card for someone" off the list. I guess this means I've definitely decided to do your Christmas to-do list. My goal is to complete the list before Christmas Day. I'm not sure if I can actually do that, but I promise to try.

Anyways, I miss you.

Love always,
Violet

CHAPTER
12

A PASSEL OF PROBLEMS

Next up for me on Mom's list was the last thing on it: "Tell a friend about this list and let them help you!" I decided I'd show Izzy, Sophia, and Daisy the letter at lunch today. On the way to the cafeteria, I stopped off at my locker to empty my backpack. I had just finished when Melanie cornered me.

"What are you doing after school today?" she asked.

"Um, what?" I glanced around the crowded hallway. Were we really going to have a conversation here in front of everyone? I already got enough grief for having the Hammer as my stepmother.

"After school today," she said. "Do you have plans?"

"I'm going to the Dusty Shelf," I said. "I want to find some books on the ancient Egyptians for my history project."

"Could you go there tomorrow instead? I really need you home this afternoon. Emma—Joey's after-school sitter—just texted me that she's starting a seasonal job at Harrison's Hardware today and can't watch him anymore." Melanie looked put out, and it dawned on me I was being told—not asked—to babysit Joey this afternoon.

Did Melanie have the right to do that?

"Some notice would have been nice," I said.

She nodded. "I agree. Emma is *completely* insensitive."

"I wasn't talking about—never mind." I sighed. "Why can't Olivia watch him?"

"Olivia has plans—she has a meeting for the student newspaper after school."

"*I* have plans," I said. "I'm going to the bookstore."

"Yes, but a meeting isn't something you can just cancel. You can go to the bookstore anytime, right?"

"Right," I repeated, slamming my locker shut. Really, what she was saying was Olivia's plans were important and mine weren't. I wondered what Dad would say if he could hear this conversation. I wondered, too, what would happen if I just said no. But I knew that would upset Dad, and besides, Addison Binchy, who's one of the biggest gossips in the sixth grade, was dawdling at her locker, listening. "I'll go straight home after school," I promised.

Melanie relaxed a little. "Thank you so much," she said.

"No problem," I answered, although I wasn't sure why she was thanking me. After all, it wasn't like she'd given me a choice.

On my way to my usual table in the cafeteria I passed Austin, who waved at me. He was looking pretty bored; Tyler and Trent, who he was sitting with, were busy playing video games on their phones.

When I sat down and began unpacking my lunch, Daisy and Sophia were eating quietly while Izzy talked. "She said they were atrocious and she couldn't believe I could stand to be seen in public wearing them. I mean, how can you not love these?"

Izzy stood up and modeled her new combat boots. They were glittery pink camouflage, with white sparkly laces.

"They're fabulous," I agreed, sliding Mom's letter out of my pocket. I figured once Izzy was done talking about her boots, I'd show it to everyone. While I was waiting, my phone pinged with a text from Austin:

I'm waiting.

Huh? I looked up and saw him grinning at me.

Waiting for what? I texted back.

For more soup! I am soooo hungry.

"Yeah, well, I wish my mom would get off my case about it," Izzy was saying. "Actually, it'd be nice if she'd stop speaking to me, period. If it's not about homework or my clothes, it's something else. Yesterday she said she was taking me to this stupid play she wants to go to—she only invited me because Carolyn is busy that day and can't go—and then she said I was going to wear a nice Christmas dress, and if I complained, I was grounded. I told her I was allergic to velvet. And lace."

"Yeah, it really sounds like you've got a passel of problems," I said, as I texted Austin back:

Whatever. I am NOT cooking for you.

When I looked up from my phone Izzy, Daisy, and Sophia were staring at me.

"Cranky, much?" Izzy said, looking irritated. "And what does 'passel' mean?"

"I'm sorry," I said. "I'm just . . . tired today. And it means 'a lot.'" I *was* sorry, but I'd heard this whole story last night, during my walkie-talkie call with Izzy. She complained so much, I got off before I could tell her about bringing soup to Austin's family.

"Passel . . ." Izzy thought about it for a second. "I like it. My mom and I have a *passel* of problems. Also, yesterday she told me I had to refold all the towels. She said the way I did it was too sloppy."

"Yeah," Sophia spoke up. "What's with moms and being neat, anyway? Yesterday my mom got annoyed because she didn't like the way I washed the dishes."

I quietly ate my lunch while Sophia talked. Sometimes I don't relate to Izzy, Sophia, or Daisy, especially when they start going on about their moms. It's like a game they play—a game every girl in school plays: Whose Mother Is the Most Annoying?

My phone pinged with another text from Austin:

Come on. I'm a growing boy. You don't want me to starve, do you?

I do if you keep sending me stupid texts, I texted right back, but I couldn't help smiling when I looked up and saw Austin grinning at me.

"Don't complain to *me*," Daisy was saying. "I would have gladly fought about dishes and towels. Yesterday Delia went on and on and *on* about Hollywood and how she wanted to move to Los Angeles and become a famous photographer. I finally opened up my notebook and started doing algebra just to get her to shut up. Of course, it didn't work, because then she started going on about how schools give out too much homework and how it's their fault kids are so stressed out all the time."

"Wow," Sophia said, wide-eyed. "She sounds really cool."

"Trust me, she's not cool," Daisy said. "She's my moth—" She stopped short when her gaze caught mine. "Oh shoot, Violet, I'm so sorry."

Everyone quieted down real fast and looked embarrassed, and I knew it was because they realized all at once they'd been caught using the M-word around me: "Mother."

"Violet," Sophia began, "we're so—"

"Don't worry about it," I said. "It's okay."

Because it was. When you're in middle school, it's normal to complain about your mom. And I'd give anything to be normal. I'd love to have an Annoying-Mom Story of my own to share, but I didn't. I just had this letter in my hands—and all of a sudden, I didn't want to show it to them.

"It's okay," I said again as I stood up from the table. "But I forgot to finish my math homework. I'll see you guys later."

I didn't want to spoil anyone's lunch with all the ugly things I was feeling, so I figured I should just take my own passel of problems somewhere else.

CHAPTER
13

NO TEXTING AT THE TABLE

On Saturday morning, we were all sitting at the table, eating the waffles Melanie had made to celebrate our first week in the new house and pretending we couldn't hear Joey as he called his dad.

"It's me, Daddy," Joey said from the hallway, because Melanie doesn't allow phone calls in the kitchen when we're eating. "Joey? Your other son? It's Saturday at eight in the morning. . . . We're supposed to talk then, remember?" He paused, and sniffed. "Anyway . . . call me back if you can."

Joey looked forlorn as he wandered back into the kitchen. Tears filled his eyes as he sat down and took a bite of his waffle.

"Forlorn"—it means "sad and lonely," and I figured it could be one of the loneliest things in the world when your dad doesn't remember to pick up the phone when you call.

Dad cleared his throat. "I'm sure he'll call back soon, Buddy," he said, shifting uncomfortably in his seat. For the time being, Dad was using our paint-splattered folding chair until he and Melanie could find a fifth matching chair for her dining set.

"Sure, he'll call back," Olivia answered. "As soon as Big-Hair Barbie lets him off his leash." Big-Hair Barbie is what Olivia calls her dad's wife.

I stared at my plate and kept quiet, but I was mad, too. I'd spent two afternoons this week watching Joey, and it was kind of nice hanging out with him. We mostly just sat at the table, and he played with his action figures while I did my homework. Every time I looked up a new word in my dictionary, I let Joey highlight it, which he thought was the coolest thing ever.

Mr. Vanderberg, Joey and Olivia's dad, lives in Texas. He sends checks every month and buys them both a pile of presents for their birthdays. As far as I can tell, the only thing he won't buy them is plane tickets so they can actually go visit him. Olivia told me it's because

Big-Hair Barbie doesn't want them around Charlie, their half-brother.

Just then my phone pinged with a text from Austin:

I'm bored!

I smiled and texted back:

So? Go DO something! Have you done any research for our Egyptian essay yet?

Besides hanging out in Miss Mallery's class, Austin and I had been texting back and forth a lot the last few days. He'd asked me a couple questions about Mom, and I found myself telling him—well, texting him—stuff I'd never told anyone else. Like how I'd read to Mom when she was in pain, or how I'd play the piano for her—even though I'm not all that great at it—when she was too tired to play herself, how I'd dragged her old record player into her room and we'd listen to Louis Armstrong and Ella Fitzgerald over and over again.

Somehow, it felt easier to text about those things than to say them out loud.

No. What's to research? They lived. They built the pyramids. Then they died. They're history! Get it, Wordnerd?

He'd started calling me Wordnerd after I told him a couple days ago about my nightly walkie-talkie chats with Izzy and our old code names. Although Izzy and I hadn't talked last night. I'd been so busy texting with Austin, I'd forgotten to switch my walkie on; so I don't know if she tried to call me.

"Can someone pass the syrup?" Dad asked. Before I could move an inch, Olivia was out of her seat and handing it to him.

"Thanks, Olivia," he said. Then his voice became stern. "Violet, how many times have I told you no texting at the table?"

The correct answer was zero. Before Melanie came along, Dad didn't care. We rarely ate our meals at the table; a lot of times it was just takeout in front of the TV, but I knew not to push it.

"I'm just finishing up," I said.

Can't talk right now. Text you later.

After I finished, I tucked my phone under my napkin.

"We'll call your dad together later," Melanie said to Joey in the steely voice she reserves for students who disrupt her class. "Trust me. He'll be there." Her voice brightened. "But in the meantime . . . I have plans for us today!"

"Really?" Joey asked, hiccupping and rubbing his eyes. "What are they?"

"I bought us all tickets to go ice-skating!"

"That sounds awesome," Olivia said.

"Yeah," I lied. The Terrible Beautiful Ache tore at my heart, though, because Mom would have known that I don't like ice-skating. Or any sports, really. But I knew Melanie was trying to make Joey feel better, and I didn't want to ruin it. "Sounds like fun," I added, and smiled. "Let me know how it goes."

Melanie frowned. "What do you mean?"

"I'll be at Caulfield Farm all day, helping out at the Christmas-tree lot."

"Oh—but I bought a ticket for you, too. I thought it would be nice if the five of us spent time together."

"Oh." Now it was my turn to frown. "Why don't you give the ticket to . . ." I was trying to think of the name of one of Olivia's friends on the baton-twirling team, but I was drawing a huge blank. Who *did* she hang out with, anyway? "Maybe Olivia can invite someone else," I said instead. I turned to her and smiled, but she glared back at me and hissed, *"Stop messing things up."*

"Messing *what* up?" I whispered. "I'm trying to do you a favor. Geez."

"You didn't tell me Violet was going to be gone all day," Melanie said to Dad, and she sounded like she was talking to a student who'd forgotten to turn in his homework. From the look on Dad's face, he noticed. And he didn't like it.

"*You* didn't tell me you'd bought tickets," he said.

"It was supposed to be a surprise."

"It is," Dad said crisply.

Dad and Melanie stared at each other until Melanie waved a hand. "Well . . . we weren't going until the afternoon, anyway." She turned to me. "I'm sure the Caulfields won't need you all day. Why don't you help out until lunchtime? We'll leave after we've eaten." She went back to her cereal, like everything was settled.

"Won't work," I said. "I'm supposed to be at the tree lot all day."

"Supposed to? That's ridiculous. I realize the Caulfields need extra help this year, but they can't expect—"

"They don't *expect* anything. I want to be there."

"Oh." Her face pinched into a frown as she understood what was happening. "So . . . this isn't something you *have* to do?" She looked back and forth between Dad and me.

"I do have to do it—I need to earn my charm." Not to mention the fact that if I spent the day at Caulfield Farm, I could cross "Volunteer for a good cause" off Mom's list.

"Earn your charm?" Melanie sounded confused, but judging by Dad's exasperated look, I was sure he had told her about the charm club. Couldn't she be bothered to remember *anything* about my life?

"It's something Violet and her friends do together," Olivia spoke up. "They have to do a task before they can put a charm on their bracelet. The next charm is a clock charm because they have to give someone the gift of their time." Olivia looked at me and shrugged. "Sophia's locker is next to mine; she told me."

Melanie and I stared at each other. It felt like we were in a boxing ring, warily circling each other, getting ready for the first round of a long fight.

"Okay," Melanie said slowly, "then if it's that important—"

"It is," I said quickly.

"—then you can take Olivia with you," she finished.

"What?" I said.

"What?" Olivia said.

"It'll give you girls a chance to get to know each other better. Maybe Olivia can get to know some of your friends, Violet."

"Mom, Violet *doesn't want* me getting to know her friends," Olivia said. Her cheeks were red with embarrassment, and I knew I'd get in a ton of trouble if I agreed with her.

"What about the ice-skating tickets you bought?" I asked. "Won't they just go to waste?"

"No—we'll just invite some of Joey's friends instead," Melanie said. "If the Caulfields need help, one extra set of hands would be helpful, right?"

I opened my mouth to tell Melanie the Caulfields didn't need *that much* extra help, but when I caught Dad's eye, he was smiling hopefully. I knew his smile would vanish if I didn't take Olivia with me.

"Sure, Olivia can come," I heard myself saying.

"Wonderful." Melanie beamed.

But across the table, Olivia was glowering at me.

CHAPTER
14

INSIDE JOKES

After Dad dropped me and Olivia off at Caulfield Farm, we started up the long driveway leading to the farmhouse. "You didn't have to say I could come," Olivia grumbled. "I don't need your charity."

"Tell that to your mother," I said. "And besides, it's not my fault if—"

"Whatever," Olivia interrupted. "We're here now. So whatever you're about to say is irrelevant."

"Irrelevant"—meaning "beside the point or unimportant." Pretty much how I feel most of the time around Melanie.

"'Irrelevant,' that's a good word," I said as I knocked on the door of the farmhouse.

Olivia smirked. "Yeah, you should put it on one of your lists in your journal."

"How do you know about my lists?" I asked.

"Hello? I live with you—you always leave it lying out on the table."

The door opened then, and Delia, Daisy's mom, said, "Hi, Violet! The other girls are already over at the tree lot. I'll walk you over there." Her gaze flicked to Olivia.

"Thanks," I said. "This is Olivia. She's . . ."

I paused. I wasn't sure how to describe Olivia, but Delia was nodding cheerfully. "She's your new stepsister, right?"

"Um . . . sure," I said, and both Olivia and I did a great job of not looking at each other.

"If you're going over there," boomed Daisy's grandmother's no-nonsense voice from somewhere in the house, "then take everyone hot drinks. It's cold out there."

"Yes, *Mother*." Delia rolled her eyes and gestured for us to follow her into the kitchen, where we started heating up a batch of the apple cider the Caulfields brew every year.

I didn't know a lot about Daisy's mom. She was younger than most other mothers and wanted everyone—including Daisy—to call her Delia. Last month she'd gone around town wearing funky glasses and bell-bottoms, but today she was dressed pretty plainly in jeans and a flannel shirt.

"Bring them some snacks, too," Grandma Caulfield said, sweeping into the kitchen. She eyed Delia reproachfully. "*They're* working hard today."

"*I'm* working hard today, too," Delia said through gritted teeth.

"What are you working on?" I asked Delia after Grandma Caulfield left the kitchen.

Delia clapped her hands together. "A new project! It's gonna be great!"

The three of us packed a picnic basket full of apples, pastries, doughnuts, and paper cups for the cider, then left the farmhouse. The Caulfields' tree lot was at the back of the farm, over by their big red barn, where rows and rows of fir trees stood waiting to be cut down. For those who didn't want to chop down their own Christmas tree, several precut trees were waiting in the barn, along with a cash register and a drink stand.

Delia led us inside the barn, where Izzy, Sophia, and Daisy were talking to Grandpa Caulfield.

"What are you doing here?" Izzy said when she caught sight of Olivia, and Sophia elbowed her in the ribs. "I mean—nice to see you."

"You too," Olivia said, and it sounded like she meant it.

Delia left, and while Olivia and I passed out doughnuts, Grandpa Caulfield told us he needed help decorating for Christmas. Every year he liked to line the fence around the tree lot with white string lights, thousands of them. The only problem was, the other eleven months of the year they sat tangled up in giant knots in huge plastic bins.

"This will take hours," Izzy complained as we hauled the bins out of the barn.

"Don't sweat it," said Jake Harris, a cute high school boy who worked part-time at the farm. "The tree lot doesn't start getting really crowded until next weekend."

"How does that make it any better?" Daisy scowled, and Jake laughed and ruffled her hair. "I hate it when he does that," she said after he stepped away to help some customers. "It's not like I'm eight years old."

Sophia and I watched Jake; he didn't realize it, but he was standing under a sprig of mistletoe someone had taped up on a wooden beam near the cash register. But Sophia and I definitely noticed.

Did I mention he was cute?

Sophia glanced over at me. "Your cheeks are red," she said.

"So what? So are yours."

We kept looking at each other until we both yelled, "Crush dibs!" at the same time.

"Crush dibs, on *Jake*?" Daisy said. "The cold must be freezing your brains solid."

Sophia, Daisy, and Izzy started trying to untangle the lights while Olivia and I poured cider into paper cups. "What's crush dibs?" Olivia asked.

"I guess it's sort of an inside joke," I said. "If Izzy, Sophia, Daisy, or I like a boy, we call 'crush dibs,' and then he's off-limits. No one else is allowed to like him."

"What happens if two of you like the same boy at the same time?" Olivia asked.

"I don't know." I shrugged. "That's never happened before."

We passed out the cups of cider, then got to work untangling lights. Sophia and I worked on the same strand, and she said, "It's been a week in the new house, right? How's it going?"

I didn't really feel like talking about Melanie, so I shrugged, and said, "It's fine."

Once we finished with our strand, we each grabbed

a different one. Soon Izzy moved next to me, and said, "Hey, what happened to you last night?"

"What do you mean?" I asked.

"I tried calling you on the walkie and you never answered."

"Oh . . . I was watching a movie," I said.

"Well, stop forgetting. That's the second time in a row."

"It is?"

"Yeah—I tried calling you Thursday night, too."

I concentrated really hard on my string of lights. Thursday night I'd been texting with Austin, too. But I didn't think Izzy would appreciate me saying I forgot to call her because I was texting with her former crush.

"Sorry," I said finally. "I'll be better next week."

We spent the next few hours untangling the lights. We were nearly finished when Sophia suddenly said, "Um, Daisy? What's your mom doing?"

Over near the cash register, Delia was digging through a big box of Christmas decorations. She hung a few ornaments on one of the trees and then began taking pictures of it.

"It's her newest thing," Daisy said, rolling her eyes. "She's convinced she can become a famous photographer."

Delia smiled and beckoned us over. "What do you

girls think?" she said, stepping back and examining the tree. "I need some creative holiday shots for my portfolio."

"Well . . . ," I said.

"It's really . . . ," Sophia began.

". . . it's kind of boring," Izzy finished, and I elbowed her in the ribs. "Ouch! You guys have to stop doing that," she said, rubbing her side. "It hurts."

"Yeah . . . I guess it's not super creative," Delia agreed, still staring at the tree.

"What if you decorated a person like a Christmas tree?" Olivia spoke up. "I saw someone play a game like that once—I think the pictures would be fun."

Delia stared at the tree for another few seconds before clapping her hands together. "That's a brilliant idea!" She picked up some tinsel and stepped closer. "Daisy?"

"No way," Daisy said, scooting backward. "You are *not* putting all that junk on me."

"Decorate Violet," Olivia said. After I shot her a dirty look she shrugged, and said, "You're the tallest. It makes sense."

"It does make sense," Izzy agreed. "Violet, step up on that wooden box over there and let us decorate you."

I really, really didn't want to do it—but it occurred to me, I could probably check "Play a Christmas game" off Mom's list, so I stepped onto the box and put my arms out.

"Thanks a lot," I said to Olivia. To the other girls I said, "There's room for two up here. Olivia is almost as tall as me—why don't you decorate both of us?"

"Thanks," Olivia said, reluctantly joining me.

"You're totally welcome," I said sweetly.

Izzy, Daisy, and Sophia got to work decorating us while Delia snapped pictures. "Smile!" Delia said to Olivia and me. "You're supposed to look like you're having fun!"

"We *are* having fun," Olivia said as Daisy began wrapping a strand of tinsel around her neck.

"Yeah, bucket loads," I added.

"You can't hang the candy canes on Violet's nose like that," Sophia said to Izzy. "It looks like she has peppermint-flavored boogers."

"That's better than original-flavored boogers," Izzy argued.

"Gross, Izzy," I said. "Take the candy canes off me."

"You're such a Grinch, Violet," Izzy said. After she removed the candy canes, she plugged a strand of lights into a nearby outlet and began wrapping them around me.

"Wait," Sophia said. "Spread your arms and legs wide—like you're in the middle of doing a jumping jack." She turned to Izzy. "What do you see?"

Izzy's eyes widened. "Sophia, you're a genius."

"What?" I said.

"You look like a human star!" Quickly, they began wrapping lights around my arms and legs until I could barely move.

"I am so getting you back for this, Izzy," I said. "You too, Sophia. One day, when you guys aren't looking, I'm going to stick mistletoe over your heads just as Tyler Jones is walking by."

"Do it. I dare you," Izzy said. "If he even *tries* to kiss either of us, I'll punch him in the face."

"Yeah?" I said. "I thought you said you were on a strict diet of forgiveness and good behavior."

Izzy shrugged. "No diet lasts forever," she said, and we all laughed.

Once everyone was finished decorating Olivia and me, Delia started taking pictures of us with her camera.

"Olivia, put your hand on Violet's shoulder and pop your hip out a bit," Delia called, taking more shots. "Good! Now put your arm around her—your parents are going to love these!"

Olivia's grin vanished, and she hesitated, her hand hovering just above my shoulder.

"Just do it, so we can this over with," I hissed.

After Delia finished, Izzy, Daisy, and Sophia quickly helped Olivia and me take off the decorations.

"Look, it's the Jacksons," Sophia said, motioning toward the front of the barn.

"Really?" Daisy squinted. "They never come this early for a tree." She turned to Izzy. "Do you want to go over there and help them?"

Izzy shook her head. "Austin's been acting really weird lately. Last night I knocked on his door to see if he wanted to play basketball, but he said he was busy."

I said nothing. The reason why Austin was busy and didn't want to play basketball last night was because we were texting back and forth while we watched the same movie on TV. (He liked it; I didn't.)

"Do you still like him?" Daisy asked.

I turned to stare at Izzy. *Say no*, I thought at her.

Wait a minute. . . . Where did *that* come from?

I thought about it and decided that since Austin and I were getting to be friends, it might be weird if Izzy still liked him. I didn't have to worry about it though, because Izzy wrinkled her nose and said, "No way—we're both over it. Besides, he's getting too tall. I don't think I could ever like someone who's that tall."

"Hey!" Jake called as he strode up to the register. He had a tree slung over his shoulder. "Can someone go over there and see if they need any help?" He gestured to the Jacksons.

"I'll go check on them," I said, and left before anyone else could volunteer.

"Hey," Austin said when he saw me approaching. He was standing, hands shoved into the pockets of his jacket, while his parents were comparing different trees. Once I was standing right in front of him, I realized Izzy was right: he *had* grown a lot this year. Now he was taller than me.

"Hi," I said. "I thought you texted me last night that you were going over to Tyler's today."

"I thought I was, too—until my parents decided we needed to put up a tree. I told them I'd rather play video games at Tyler's, but they insisted. I don't know why they're making such a big deal about it."

"I do," I blurted. Austin looked confused, and I added, "It's because your mom's leaving on her trip soon."

He still didn't look convinced, but I knew I was right. The first Christmas after Mom got sick, she and Dad went all out: a bigger tree, more presents, a huge Christmas dinner. I overheard Mom tell Dad she just wanted to make the most of whatever time she had left. I knew it wasn't the same with Austin's family, but I was still pretty sure that with Mrs. Jackson leaving for New York soon, they wanted to celebrate the holiday season while they were all still together.

"I guess," Austin said finally. "But I'd still rather be playing Xbox."

We waited silently while Mr. and Mrs. Jackson continued to look at trees. "So," I said, "have you thought anymore about our Egyptian project?"

"Not really—but I guess we'd better get started soon. I'm so excited!" he said, doing a perfect impersonation of Miss Mallery.

"Excited about what?" Izzy asked, and we both jumped. Neither of us had heard her come up behind us.

"Um . . . inside joke, I guess," Austin said.

Izzy glanced at me and I shrugged.

"I guess you had to be there," I said.

"Oh, okay." Izzy laughed, but she didn't actually look that happy.

CHAPTER 15

A CHAIN OF TEXTS

After the Jacksons left, the tree lot got busier. The rest of the day went fast, and when the sky had turned pinkish gray, Grandma Caulfield appeared and invited us all inside for dinner. We followed her back into the farmhouse, and when we entered the kitchen, we were greeted with the scents of garlic and herbs and onions.

"I made spaghetti and a meatless sauce," Grandma Caulfield said. "Violet, you're a vegetarian, right?"

I swallowed a lump in my throat. "Right," I said, touched that she remembered and didn't make a big deal about it. Melanie always seemed irritated or personally insulted when I didn't eat everything she cooked.

"You girls are welcome to spend the night, too," Grandma Caulfield said.

"Violet and I can't," Olivia said. "The baton-twirling team is performing at Dandelion High's football game later." She turned to me. "Your dad is supposed to be picking us up soon so we can go."

"He is?" I said. No one told *me* that. I pulled out my phone and texted Dad:

Can I spend the night at the Caulfields'? Please? I don't want to go to the football game.

"I'm starving," Daisy said. Before she could grab a plate, Sophia said, "Wait." She reached into her pocket and pulled out her clock charm. "This first."

Each of us pulled our charms from our pockets. "We have earned our charm," Izzy said solemnly, and the four of us hooked the tiny clock to our bracelets while Olivia watched.

"Your charm club seems like a lot of fun," Olivia whispered to me as Grandma Caulfield passed out plates piled with spaghetti.

After we finished eating, the doorbell rang and Delia went to answer it. She returned with Aunt Mildred, who was carrying four tiny boxes from Charming Trinkets.

"More charms?" Daisy asked.

"More charms," Aunt Mildred confirmed, and Izzy and Daisy high-fived.

"Would you like some coffee?" Grandma Caulfield asked, and Aunt Mildred nodded.

"I thought I would give you your next round of charms now." Aunt Mildred shot a tentative look at Olivia, who said, "Don't mind me; I've been wondering how your club works."

While Olivia looked on curiously, Aunt Mildred passed around the boxes, and we opened them. Inside were two charms. The first was a tiny gingerbread house. It was gold and brown with multicolored bits of glass speckled on the roof. The second charm was a tiny Santa hat.

"The Santa-hat charm is for Secret Santas." Aunt Mildred produced a tiny red velvet bag. "Pick a name out of here, and that's who you buy a present for." She glanced at Daisy. "See? I told you we'd have fun this time around."

Izzy went first. She pulled a small paper square from the bag and frowned. "What happens if you pick your own name?"

"Put it back and pick another one."

Izzy did, and then it was my turn. I drew Izzy's name, which I was glad about, because I really wanted to get her something nice this year, now that we were friends again.

After Sophia and Daisy picked a name, Aunt Mildred said, "The gingerbread-house charm is for next weekend—you'll be making them together." Aunt Mildred looked at Izzy. "Your parents have already agreed to host Friday night, and everyone can spend the night if you want."

I surreptitiously slid Mom's letter and list from my pocket and looked at it under the table.

"Surreptitiously"—it means "done by secret" or "acting in a stealthy way." I guess I'd been sort of secretive about the letter. I still hadn't told Izzy, Daisy, and Sophia about it—there just never seemed to be a good time. But sitting in the warm glow of the Caulfields' kitchen, it seemed that the right time was right now.

"Do you think your Christmas tree will be up by then?" I asked Izzy.

"Probably, why?"

"Because I have to do a sleepover under a Christmas tree." Slowly, as they listened quietly with wide-eyed stares, I began to tell them about finding Mom's letter and about her list. By the time I was finished, Sophia was fighting tears, and Izzy and Daisy looked grave. Olivia didn't look all that surprised, and I wondered if Dad had said something to her about Mom's letter.

"I'm so sorry, Violet," Daisy said.

"It's not a bad thing," I said. "I'm glad I found the letter."

"I can't imagine what it's like to lose a mother so young," Aunt Mildred said. "But I do know what it's like to lose someone long before they should've been lost. And if you're lucky enough to hear from them after they've passed, you've got to take advantage of it." She had a far-away look in her eyes. I was pretty sure she was thinking of Jack Whippie; her husband of only a few hours, before he was killed in a car crash.

"Can we read the letter?" Izzy asked, reaching for it.

"No." Sophia laid her hand on Izzy's. "Something like that should be private. . . . But could we see the list, though?"

"Sure." I handed the list to Sophia. Izzy and Daisy gathered around her, and everyone read quietly.

"Are you going to do it?" Sophia asked.

"Finish the list?" I asked, and she nodded. "Yeah. I'm going to try to finish everything before Christmas. But I haven't gotten that far yet."

"Good, then it's settled." Sophia took out her cell phone and snapped a picture of the list. "We're going to help you finish it." She looked up suddenly. "If you're okay with that. I mean, I could delete the picture, if it's not okay."

"No," I said, swallowing a lump in my throat. "It's okay."

I stared around the table; Izzy, Daisy, Sophia, and Aunt Mildred stared back at me, smiling, and I realized I felt more comfortable, more at home, here at Caulfield Farm, eating dinner with the Charm Girls, than I probably ever would at Melanie's too-small dinner table. When I glanced over at Olivia, she had a strange expression on her face, and I wondered if she knew what I was thinking.

"Coffee's done," Grandma Caulfield said. She sat down at the table and handed Aunt Mildred a steaming cup. Then Delia announced that she wanted to clean out her closet and get rid of some things. "Do any of you want to help?" she asked me, Izzy, Sophia, Daisy, and Olivia. "You can have some of my old clothes, if you want."

"Definitely," Izzy said immediately. "Do you have any long skirts you're giving away?"

Izzy, Sophia, Daisy, and I followed Delia back to her room. Olivia hung back, and as I left the room I heard her ask Aunt Mildred, "Do you pick out the charms, or does Izzy tell you what to buy?"

Delia's room was huge. Besides having her own bathroom and a big walk-in closet, there was a four-poster bed covered with a plaid quilt, a few squashy armchairs in front of a fireplace, a mirror in the corner, and posters of

Delia's favorite rock bands plastered on the walls. It didn't seem like a mom's room—more like a big sister's.

"Wow," Sophia said as we all ducked inside Delia's closet. "You have so *many* clothes."

I like clothes, and I like trying them on, but rifling through Delia's stuff reminded me of the day Dad and I finally donated Mom's clothes to the Goodwill, and the Terrible Beautiful Ache hit me so hard I wasn't sure I could keep standing.

"Violet?" Daisy said. "Are you okay?"

"I'm fine," I said. After all, it had been a year since we'd gotten rid of Mom's clothes; I felt stupid telling everyone it was bothering me now. "I think I'll just watch—I probably just ate too much." I made it over to the fireplace and collapsed into an armchair. The warmth I had felt as we ate spaghetti together began to evaporate.

As I watched them, it was hard not to think about other things, like the way Mom's clothes smelled like her. All the birthday cards she'd saved from Dad and me over the years—we'd found them tucked in her dresser drawer. Her T-shirt that had a picture of the Golden Gate Bridge on it that I kept and sometimes still wore to bed.

A text came in then from Austin:

How's it going?

Okay. Everyone's helping Daisy's mom clean out her closet. Not really into it.

Tell me about it. My parents are decorating the tree and being all kissy-faced. It's disgusting. Usually, my mom yells at my dad to put more lights on the tree while he says a bunch of bad words.

Dad called me then, but I sent the call to voice mail so I could text Austin back:

Yeah. Nothing like a little family fight to start the holidays right.

Ha! You're a poet, and you don't even know it!

"What's so funny?" Izzy asked.

"What?" I looked up, startled. Izzy was dressed in one of Delia's colorful skirts; the three of them had started trying on her clothes while I'd been texting with Austin.

"You're laughing. Who are you texting?"

I felt weird telling her I was texting Austin, so I said, "No one. Just someone from history class."

"Violet?" Grandma Caulfield came into the room. "Your step . . ." she paused in midsentence. "Melanie is here for you and Olivia," she finished, just as a text came in from Dad:

Can't do a sleepover tonight, Champ. Sorry. We're outside waiting for you.

I jammed my phone into my pocket. "I guess I'll see you guys later," I muttered to Izzy, Daisy, and Sophia.

"You didn't have to just show up like that," I said when I got in Melanie's minivan. Dad was driving, and Olivia had just settled herself in the back row next to Joey. "It was embarrassing."

"No one was trying to embarrass you, Champ," Dad said. "We decided to go to the football game at Dandelion High tonight. I know Olivia told you that."

"I hate football, Dad. You *know* that. You guys could have gone without me."

"We're all going together," Melanie said. "The whole . . ."

Family. The word was there, like a bad smell in the air, even if she didn't say it.

"You should have at least called first and asked me if I wanted to go," I said.

Dad was silent, but Melanie twisted around to look at me. "No, Violet. I should *not* have. Because you are not in charge. You're a child, not an adult, and you don't make the decisions. Olivia's baton-twirling team was invited to perform during halftime. She's really excited about it, and we're all going to support her."

"I took Olivia to the farm and hung out with her all day like you asked me to. Now I can't have a little time alone with my friends because I have to go see her stupid baton-twirling routine?"

"Way to be a jerk, Violet," Olivia said.

"It's not stupid," Melanie began. "And I don't appreciate—"

"Dad," I said, ignoring her, "why is what Olivia wants to do more important than what I want to do?"

"Nobody is more important than anybody else," Dad said. "We just wanted to spend the night together. As a family," he added firmly, looking at Melanie.

"No," I said. "What you really decided is that Olivia's plans and her friends are more important than mine."

We drove the rest of the way in silence, and it occurred to me that I didn't really belong anywhere. Not in Melanie's minivan and not in the Caulfield's kitchen, either. I pulled out my cell phone, just as another text came in from Austin:

Dad just plugged the tree in and it blew a fuse and the whole house lost power. Christmas sucks.

As I read, I imagined a chain of our texts stretching from me in the silent car all the way across town to Austin in his dark living room, connecting us. I decided to answer him back, even though I knew Melanie hates texting in the car. Because lately, the only time I felt normal was when Austin and I were texting.

CHAPTER
16

A THIN WALL
OF GLASS

Dear Mom,

I wasn't planning on writing you another letter, but writing the first one made me feel better, so I thought I'd try it again. Tonight I ate dinner with Izzy, Sophia, and Daisy. I put another charm on my bracelet, and Aunt Mildred gave me two more to earn. I told the Charm Girls about your list, and they decided to help me with it. After I showed the girls your list, everything felt light and sweet, like eating the best shortbread cookies you ever tasted. But the feeling didn't last long, and after a while I went back to feeling how I always feel: like a thin wall of glass separates me from everyone else. On one side was Izzy, Sophia, and Daisy, and they were happy and laughing and trying on clothes and having a wonderful time. I could see them, but I couldn't join them. And then it ended up not mattering anyway, because Melanie made me leave so I could go to a stupid football game.

This Christmas is turning out to be tougher than I thought. Last year, everyone would ask me how I was doing and they'd talk about you, which was hard, but it felt right. This year, hardly anyone has mentioned you, and that doesn't feel right at all. I wish you were here so I could talk to you. I know I said I'd try to finish the list before Christmas, but I don't think Dad will have time to drive us to the snow this month.

I'll keep working on your list, and let you know how it's going.

Love always,
Violet

CHAPTER 17

POPCORN BALL

Normally, I love school projects. I know some people—like Izzy—think that's nerdy, but I like going to the library, and I like doing research. But I've never done a school project with a boy before.

On Monday afternoon, Austin and I were supposed to meet after school at the Dusty Shelf to finally start figuring out what to do about our Egyptian project. After my last class ended, I went to the girls' bathroom and brushed my hair. I was reapplying my lip gloss when Addison Binchy and Penelope Perkins walked in.

". . . and then she said my essay lacked depth," Addison was saying. "Can you believe that?"

"The Hammer is my least favorite teacher," Penelope agreed. "I wish they'd just fire her—Oh, hi, Violet." Her face changed, and I saw it, the exact moment she realized Melanie was my stepmom. "Hey—I didn't mean—"

"Forget it," I said, capping my lip gloss. "You think *you* don't like her? Try living with her. It's a nightmare." I meant it, every single word, especially when I thought about the two hours I'd spent shivering on the bleachers at Dandelion High after she made me leave Daisy's house, just so we could watch Olivia's baton team perform for maybe five minutes during halftime.

I also had to admit that it felt nice talking with two girls—even if one of them was Addison Binchy—about my stepmother. Normal. And normal wasn't something I'd had a lot of lately.

"Seriously," Addison said, taking a brush from her backpack and running it through her hair. "Didn't you get kicked out of her class a couple months ago?"

"Yeah, I'm in Miss Carter's class now." A month after school started, I'd stolen Melanie's set of school keys. It was the worst thing I've ever done, but it was the only thing I could think of to get myself out of her class.

"Lucky you," Penelope said. "I heard Miss Carter is way easier."

"She is," I said. "And way nicer."

Addison and Penelope finished brushing their hair, and left. The toilet behind me flushed, the stall door opened . . . and Olivia walked out and began washing her hands.

"Oh, hi," I said. From the hard look in her eyes, I knew she'd heard everything, and surprisingly, I felt bad. "I'm sorry," I said. "It's just that I get tired of everyone talking about Dad and Melanie and—"

"Don't you think *I* get tired of it, too?" Olivia interrupted. She was scrubbing her hands so hard, I thought she'd rub the skin right off. "Don't you think that maybe, just maybe, you're not the only one who gets grief for being related to the Hammer?"

Um . . . total honesty? No, I *hadn't* thought about it. Not even once. In fact, I tried real hard to think about Olivia as little as possible. But I couldn't exactly tell her that.

"Except for *me*," she continued, "it started the very first day of class." She spread her arms wide, "Welcome to Dandelion Middle—we all *hate* your mother."

That sounded terrible, and I was about to tell her so when she added, "You know, my mom was really unhappy before she met your dad." She ripped a paper towel from the dispenser. "She used to hide in the kitchen and cry all the time."

Suddenly, I was mad. So mad I wanted to stomp my feet. Or take a swing at Olivia or slam the bathroom door, and I wasn't even sure why. Maybe it was the thought of Melanie crying in front of a pile of dirty dishes or the fact that at lunch today Izzy, Sophia, and Daisy were talking about how much fun they'd had spending the night at Caulfield Farm.

"Oh yeah?" I said. "Well, my mom used to cry a lot, too. Then she died."

I purposely didn't look at Olivia as I brushed past her and slammed out of the bathroom.

When I walked into the Dusty Bookshelf, Scooter was at the cash register, helping customers. "Violet! I'm delighted to see you. I'll be with you in a minute. Bob is in the back, and he is in desperate need of a good petting."

Bob is Scooter's orange tabby cat—the hugest, fattest one I've ever seen—and he likes books. I found him in the literature section, where he was sitting imperiously on top of a bookshelf, staring down at a couple who were examining books by Ernest Hemingway.

"Oh, what a cute kitty," the girl said.

In response, Bob twitched his tail and yawned.

I sat down on a comfy couch, and as soon as the couple

left, Bob jumped and landed on the ground with a loud *thud*, then climbed into my lap and started purring. I really like coming here, where it's quiet and I can be by myself.

I thought about texting Olivia and apologizing, but I just couldn't bring myself to do it.

The truth is, in the bathroom back there, I used Mom's death as a bat and smacked it across Olivia's stunned face. I knew if Mom really could see me now, she wouldn't be proud. But I was so sick of people talking about Dad and Melanie, and I was embarrassed to admit that I hadn't ever realized things probably weren't always easy for Olivia, either.

"Someone's missed you," Scooter said as Bob bumped his head against my hand until I started petting him. "Anything I can help you with today before I leave?"

"Leave?" I said. "Where are you going?"

Scooter grinned. "Got myself a hot date with Mildred. She has consented to letting me take her out for an after-noon slice of pie at the Kaleidoscope."

"That sounds nice," I said. "Austin Jackson and I need to write an essay on the ancient Egyptians. Do you have any books I can buy?"

"No—but I have a couple you can *have*, free of charge. Let me just go find them."

While he was looking through the shop, Austin arrived. "Wow, what a fat cat," he said when he saw Bob.

In response, Bob lifted his head to glare at him.

"Geez—talk about a death stare." Austin plopped down next to me. "What's wrong?" he asked. "You look kind of bummed."

"Nothing," I answered. "Just family stuff." My voice broke a little bit on the word "family." On the idea that I was going to grow up; I was going to meet people who had never known Mom; and for years when I said the word "family," they would think not only of Dad, but of Melanie and Olivia.

I'd never thought about that before.

"What's it like, having a stepsister and stepbrother all of a sudden?" Austin asked. "I mean, I've always wondered what it would be like to have siblings, since I'm an only child."

"I'm still an only child," I said quickly, although I knew things were different now.

"Okay," Austin said. I think he could tell I didn't want to talk about it. He drummed his fingers on the couch. "So . . . any ideas for our project?"

"Scooter's finding us books so we can do research for our essay," I said as I continued to pet Bob.

"Books?" Austin frowned. "Why can't we get all our sources off the Internet?"

"Because, young man," Scooter said, returning with a stack of old textbooks, "the Internet is no substitute for scholarly research."

"Meow." Bob agreed.

"Oh," Austin said, sitting up straighter, "you're totally right."

After that, we stopped by Don's Donuts so Austin could purchase a bunch of jelly rolls, which he ate on the way home. It felt strange talking to him face-to-face as we walked to my house; most of our conversations were usually via text. While we walked, I found myself telling him a few things about what it was like living with Olivia and Joey, how loud they were in the mornings, how mad it made me every time Mr. Vanderberg missed a phone call with Joey, how annoying it was that Olivia always blasted her iPod, especially since I can't stand her music.

At home, Joey was sitting in the rocker on the front porch, his lips puffed out in a pout. And all of a sudden I realized: It was Monday. I was supposed to go home right after school, because Melanie needed someone to watch Joey, and Olivia had an Eco Club meeting, and, of course, that was more important than whatever I was doing.

"Where *were* you?" he demanded as Austin and I walked up to the porch.

"Working on a school project." I bent down till I was eye level with him. "I'm so sorry. Forgive me?"

Joey seemed to consider. "Can I have a snack?" he asked.

"Whatever you want," I said, and he sprang off the rocker. "Who are you?" he asked Austin while I unlocked the front door. "Are you Violet's boyfriend?"

"Joey," I said quickly, "why don't you go into the living room and I'll get you your food."

"I could eat, too," Austin said.

"You're hungry? You just had a ton of doughnuts." No wonder he kept growing, I thought as we headed for the kitchen. He never stopped eating.

"How about some popcorn?" I asked.

"Sounds good to me."

Austin joined Joey in the living room while I stuck a bag of popcorn in the microwave. While I was waiting, I texted Olivia: I'm sorry.

She texted back immediately: Whatever.

I decided against texting her again. I put away my cell and pulled out Mom's letter. I kept it on me at all times; I'd read it so much, it was starting to look worn. I wished I could talk to her about my fight with Olivia. I also wished she'd left me more than a Christmas to-do list.

I wished she'd left me instructions on how to live life without her.

"What's that?" Austin said, coming back into the kitchen.

"It's a letter from my mother," I said.

Austin's eyes widened. "How is that possible?"

So far, the only person I'd let read Mom's actual letter was Coco Martin, and right then I realized I wanted to talk about it with someone. "Dad was supposed to give it to me last year, but he forgot. Here."

I handed the letter to Austin and concentrated on pouring the popcorn into two bowls while he read.

"Wow," he said when he finished. "This is awesome. But you haven't crossed many things off the list yet."

"Yeah, I know. I just haven't been into Christmas much this year."

"Do you have thread and a couple of needles?" he asked suddenly. "Let's string popcorn garland together. We've already got the popcorn right here. Let's just do it, and we can cross it off your list."

"Austin." I sighed. "That's really nice, but we *need* to study."

"We will! Come on, let's do one small strand, cross it off the list, and then we'll start on the project."

"Well . . . I guess one strand won't take too long." I found some thread and needles, and we got to work on making popcorn garland in the living room. Joey helped us, but it took longer than it should have—Austin ate four pieces for every one that he strung, and I had to pop another batch.

"There!" he said, tying up the end of the string. "Popcorn garland, done! Check it out, and check it off!" He pumped his fist.

I laughed and picked up one of Melanie's red pens she uses for grading and crossed "String popcorn garland" off the list. It felt good.

"Want to play basketball?" he said.

"We really should start working on our project. And I don't like basketball."

"No. I mean, popcorn basketball." He tossed a piece into the air and caught it with his mouth.

"That's not a real game," I said.

"It's definitely a real game. Open your mouth and see how many you can catch." He grinned. "I'll bet I can catch more than you."

He tossed three pieces into the air and caught them. "See if you can beat that."

We started competing to see who could catch the

most. Austin hit a high of ten pieces in a row before shouting, "Teams! Let's see how many we could do together!"

He moved back a couple of spots and opened his mouth. I tossed a piece at him, and he caught it. Three more, and then he missed. "That was a lousy throw," he said.

"That was a lousy catch."

"We'll see who's a lousy catcher." He grabbed a handful of popcorn. "Back up, Hotshot. Now it's your turn."

I was a lousy catcher. Austin kept tossing popcorn at me, and I kept missing. He began throwing them underhanded, like pitching a softball, and then I started doing a better job. While we played, I felt like that wall of glass that always seemed to separate me from everyone else thinned out and went soft, like water. Like I could reach right through it, and grab onto the other side, where things were warm and shiny.

"What's going on here?" Melanie stood in the doorway, arms crossed, looking decidedly unhappy. "The floor is a mess."

I looked down. Popcorn littered the carpet, like it had snowed inside. "We'll clean it up," I said quickly.

"We were working on our Egyptian report," Austin said.

"I can see that," Melanie said. "Looks like you got a lot done."

Austin looked down and my cheeks flamed up. "It was our first day working together. We were just trying to figure out what to do," I said.

"I also got a call from Mrs. Graves, the neighbor across the street," Melanie continued. "She told me that Joey spent an hour sitting on that front porch before you showed up."

"I'm sorry, I just—I forgot."

Melanie stared hard at me a bit longer before waving her hand. "Fine. But your study session is done for today." She spun on her heel and left the room.

"I'm so sorry," I said as I walked Austin to the door.

"It's okay. It's not a successful day if I haven't irritated the Hammer at least once." We both laughed, and Austin added, "Seriously—it was fun hanging out." He smiled at me, but it was a shy, weird smile. "Text you later, Word-nerd?"

"Sure—text you later," I said.

It wasn't until after I'd shut the door that I thought about his smile and the look in his eye when he called me Wordnerd that I wondered: *Was Austin* flirting *with me?*

CHAPTER

18

THE BEST
PRESENTS

When I'm confused about something, I like to make a list and see if I can figure it out. So the next afternoon, when Joey and I were sitting at the kitchen table, instead of doing my homework, I made a list about Austin:

REASONS WHY I THINK AUSTIN LIKES ME
- HE TEXTS ME ALL THE TIME. SERIOUSLY—ALL. THE. TIME.
- HE'S STARTED SAVING ME A SEAT NEXT TO HIM IN MISS MALLERY'S CLASS.

- I'M PRETTY SURE I'M THE ONLY ONE
  HE'S TOLD ABOUT HIS MOM MAYBE
  GOING TO LIVE IN NEW YORK.

When we were texting late last night, I asked him if he'd told Tyler Jones or Trent Walker, and he said they're immature and he can't talk to them. When I asked him who he can talk to, he texted back: Just You.

At lunch, whenever I look over at his table, I notice him looking at me.

I notice him in the hallways at school all the time now. I guess you could say we spend a lot of time noticing each other.

Big Conclusion? I'm pretty sure he likes me.

Potential Bigger Conclusion? I think I might like him back.

Just then my cell pinged with a text from Austin.

I've been thinking . . .

I smiled—I liked the idea that Austin had been thinking about me, right when I was thinking about him. I waited, but when he didn't send another text, I sent one of my own:

You've been thinking? Congratulations, I KNEW it was bound to happen!

Next to me, Joey had been coloring with his markers. On a yellow piece of construction paper, he'd drawn a picture of what I thought was supposed to be Dad and Melanie standing next to a Christmas tree.

"That's a great picture," I told him. When he didn't answer, I looked over and saw him sniffing. "Is everything okay?" I asked.

He wiped his eyes. "I don't know what to get Mitch for Christmas."

"I'm sure whatever you get him he'll like. Dads are easy like that."

Joey shook his head. "Once I made my dad a necklace and he never wore it. I found it in the trash."

The more I heard about Olivia and Joey's dad, the more I didn't like him. And I knew my own dad would have proudly worn the necklace everywhere.

"I only have six dollars. That's not enough to get anything," Joey continued morosely.

"Morosely"—it means "characterized by or expressing gloom."

Gloom was descending like a black sheet over both of us, so I said, "Sometimes the best Christmas presents don't come from a store." I was pretty sure I'd heard that in a book somewhere, and when I thought back to the letters Mom used to write me, I realized it was true. "My dad would love anything you gave him," I added. "Think about what you'd really like to give him. Something that doesn't cost money."

While Joey thought about it, my phone pinged with another text from Austin:

Sorry about that. My dad was asking me a question. . . . Anyway, I was thinking. I want to help you with your mom's list. I have ideas for some stuff we could do.

At that, my heart started spinning cartwheels.

You're on!

It's really true, I thought. Sometimes the best presents don't come from the store. I think Joey agreed with me, because as I put my phone away and pulled out my homework, he said, "I think I have an idea for a good present."

"What is it?" I asked.

"You'll see" was all he'd say.

I found out what he meant later, at dinner. While we ate, he was squirming around, looking like he was going to burst with excitement.

"Joey, stop playing with your food," Melanie said after he'd used his mashed potatoes to build a snowman.

"Do you have to wait until Christmas to give someone their present?" he asked.

"Not necessarily," Melanie said. "I get presents from students all throughout December."

I found it hard to believe that students actually bought the Hammer presents, but Joey smiled widely. "Okay, then I'm going to give Mitch his Christmas present now!" He leaped out of his seat and faced Dad. "Starting right now, I'm going to call you 'Dad'!"

The table went silent. Dad's eyes grew misty, and Melanie brought a napkin to her face. Her shoulders shook slightly.

"You want to call me 'Dad'?" Dad repeated, glancing briefly at Melanie. "Are you sure, Buddy?"

Joey nodded seriously. "My real dad won't care, and I've decided you're a better dad than he is, anyway."

Melanie gave a muffled sob, and Olivia stared blankly at her plate. It felt indecent, almost, watching them. Little kids can say the most honest things. They don't know they're supposed to pretend everything is fine. That it's perfectly normal that Joey's dad is never available for Saturday morning or Wednesday evening phone calls.

"That's a really sweet idea," Melanie said, a quiver in her voice.

"It wasn't my idea," Joey answered. "It was Violet's."

"It was? Really?"

It felt uncomfortable, the way Melanie was staring at me. Like I was a rock star or an angel or something. Meanwhile, Olivia didn't look too happy, and I had a funny feeling in my stomach, like I'd let her down somehow. After all, I knew she liked my dad—liked him a lot, in fact, judging by the way she was always kissing up to him—but I'd never heard her call him anything other than "Mitch."

"It wasn't exactly my idea," I said quickly. "I just said sometimes the best presents don't cost money." I wanted so badly to say something snarky, but I also knew I couldn't mess this up for Dad or Joey. I knew Dad loved Joey, and in my own way, I was starting to love him, too. He deserved a good dad, and if his own dad couldn't do the job, I was glad he had mine.

Dad stared at Melanie, who nodded once. "Okay, Buddy, that's a wonderful present. Thank you so much."

"No problem—Dad," Joey said, and the two of them high-fived.

Olivia and I stared at each other. It felt like something was shifting around us. Like a small piece of our new pattern was falling into place. I didn't know how I felt about it. But I was willing to bet if I could have put it into words, Olivia was the only one who would've understood.

CHAPTER
19

GRIEF AND GHOSTS

On Wednesday after school, I was standing in the hallway applying lip gloss when Melanie walked in, and said, "Where are you going?"

"Over to Austin's," I answered as I checked my reflection in the mirror. "We need to work on our Egyptian project."

She frowned. "When did you tell me this?"

"I told Dad last night after dinner," I said.

Melanie ran a hand through her hair. "Violet—look, I realize you're used to coming and going as you please, but that's going to have to change. We need to all start checking in with one another. That means telling your Dad *and* me."

"Okay," I said, fighting hard to stay calm. Just because

Dad was now officially "Joey's dad" did not mean I thought of Melanie as my mother. "Would you rather I not go? I'm not really excited to spend the afternoon studying," I added, which was true, but my heart was doing jumping jacks at the idea of seeing Austin.

"How much work have you gotten done on the project?"

"Well . . . so far, none," I admitted. Before she could get upset about that, I added, "But we'll catch up, I promise."

Melanie sighed. "Okay—you can go. But come back in a couple hours. Your dad is picking up a Christmas tree from Caulfield Farm after he leaves work, and we're going to decorate it before dinner."

Sometimes grief feels like a ghost—the ghost of all the Christmas pasts that I had with Mom—and it's moments like these where they rise up and make the Terrible Beautiful Ache inside me squeeze tight. Last year during Black Christmas, Dad and I hadn't gotten a tree, and even though I knew decorating one was on Mom's list, it still felt wrong to be doing it without her.

"Sure," I said, my voice catching a little as I zipped up my jacket. "That sounds great."

"Violet." Melanie's voice softened. "I know—"

"Don't worry about it," I said, opening the front door. "I'll be home in time."

20

ICE BLOCKING

It had rained earlier in the day, and the afternoon was chilly and gloomy as I turned onto Austin's street, but my heart was beating so fast, I wasn't all that cold. I've had crushes on boys before; I get them all the time. To me, a crush just means that you like a boy. Like, *like* him like him. You may not even know his name, but you can still like him. It still counts. But I've never had a crush on a boy who was already someone I knew, someone who was already my friend.

The Jacksons live next door to Izzy, so I decided to stop at her house first. I figured now was a good time to tell her about my crush. I'd meant to tell her when we talked on our walkie-talkies last night, but I'd forgotten to turn mine on again because I'd been texting back and forth with Austin.

I knocked on the door, and Grandma Bertie answered. "Oh, hello, Violet," she said.

"Is Izzy here?" I asked.

Grandma Bertie shook her head. "No, she's gone to Dandelion Lake with her dad. Crazy, if you ask me—it's way too cold to be kayaking in this weather. Do you want to come in? I'm afraid Mildred isn't here, either. She's out on a date with Scooter McGee." She lowered her voice and added. "That's the third time this week!"

"No, thank you," I said. "I couldn't stay long anyway—I'm supposed to go over to Austin's to work on a school project."

I headed next door, and as I was walking up the driveway, the front door opened—like he'd been waiting for me—and Austin appeared. "Ready?" he asked.

"To work on our project, you mean?"

"Nope," he said, without missing a beat. "Today we are in a homework-free zone. We're crossing something off your mom's list. Come on."

"Austin, I think we really need to start," I protested as I followed him to his garage, where he pulled a funny-shaped sled off a shelf. "Don't you want to get a good grade?"

"Don't *you* want to have a little fun?" He propped the sled up against a couple boxes. "My dad made this himself."

"It's awesome," I said. "What are we doing with it?"

"Duh. We're going sledding—it was on your mom's list, remember?"

"Duh—of course I remember. But don't you need, you know, *actual snow* to go sledding?"

"Nope. Because we're not sledding over snow. All we need is a hill and some mud. We're going ice-blocking."

I blinked. "Ice what?"

"Ice-blocking." He flipped the sled over to show me two deep inserts in the back side. "You put a big block of ice here and here. Dad keeps them in our freezer." He flipped the sled back over. "And you take it to the top of a hill and go sailing down. Your mom's list didn't specifically say *snow* sledding, so today we're sledding over mud. Ice-blocking."

"It looks dangerous," I said, examining the sled. "Can you actually steer it?"

"Who needs to steer it? You just go straight down."

"Well . . . I don't know. We really should start work on our project."

Austin rolled his eyes. "There's still plenty of time to get the project done. Have a little fun, Wordnerd."

Hearing Austin call me "Wordnerd" felt a lot different

than when Izzy did. And what could it hurt, anyway? I really did want to cross more items off Mom's list, and unless Dad was going to suddenly take a day off during the busiest season of the year, ice-blocking was probably the only way I'd get any sledding done before Christmas.

I stashed my backpack in the garage while Austin wrapped up the blocks of ice in rags and stuck them on an old red wagon. We set off for Poppy Hill, both of us taking turns either pulling the wagon or carrying the sled. In the spring, Poppy Hill produces a carpet of wildflowers, but in the winter it's frosted with dead grass and, thanks to this afternoon's rain, a ton of slippery mud. We climbed the hill, and after he'd inserted the ice and righted the sled, he said, "The trick is to not fall off."

"Sounds like a fancy strategy," I said, and he shot me a dirty look.

Austin hopped onto the sled and went careening down the muddy hill until he came to a stop at the bottom.

"Your turn," he said, after he dragged the sled back up the hill.

I couldn't remember the last time I'd been sledding—Dad hadn't wanted to take any day trips to the snow the last couple of years.

"Ready?" Austin asked after I'd settled myself. I gave

him a thumbs-up. "Okay. One . . . Two . . . Three!" He pushed the sled, and soon I was flying down the hill, my stomach plunging, icy wind whipping at my face. Something sweet and fizzy bubbled up inside me—like drinking the best can of cherry cola in the world.

"That was awesome!" I yelled when I reached the bottom.

"I know!" Austin scrambled down and helped me carry the sled back up the hill.

"Exhilarated"—it can mean "to feel cheerful and excited." That's exactly how I felt as we continued taking turns going down the hill. The wind was in my hair, my heart was pumping, and I felt happier than I had in ages. I forgot about Gray Christmas and the Terrible Beautiful Ache, and wished I could stay on the sled forever.

When the sun was setting, we decided to go down the hill together. Austin hopped onto the back of the sled, and I settled myself in front of him.

"Ready?" he asked.

"Ready!"

He pushed off, but this time we veered slightly to the left, and halfway down the ice block struck the side of a rock. The sled upended and tumbled through the air, dumping Austin and me into the mud.

"Ow," I said, rubbing my shoulder. "Apparently steering *does* matter."

"Apparently, it does." Austin groaned and rolled over. "Are you okay?"

He was on his side, staring down at me, and I could feel his breath on my face.

"I'm fine," I said.

"Good." He sniffed. "Do you smell licorice?"

"Um . . . I think that's my lip gloss." I was glad it was dark, because my cheeks were probably as red as a Santa suit.

"Oh." He glanced down at my lips and hesitated . . . then flopped over onto his back. I felt a huge wave of relief, because for the tiniest, craziest second, I thought he might try to kiss me.

I mean, don't get me wrong. I hope to kiss a boy one day. But I sort of hope it will be a day when I'm all dressed up and standing somewhere pretty, like a beach or a ballroom. Not lying in the mud with leaves stuck in my hair, a rock digging into my back on a cold December night. And definitely not before I tell Izzy, Sophia, and Daisy I have a real, true-blue crush on my hands. Because isn't that half the fun of having a crush, being able to tell your friends about it? I was glad Izzy didn't like Austin anymore, and I hoped it wouldn't be weird for her that I liked him now.

"Think we should get going?" I asked.

"Yeah," Austin said, but he didn't sound too eager to leave. "Hey, Violet, can I ask you something?"

"Yeah, what?"

"Do you ever sometimes feel like the world is spinning?"

"The world *is* spinning," I said. "Haven't you ever studied astronomy?"

"No, that's not what I mean." I turned and saw he was staring up at the darkening sky, completely serious. "I mean, like, since middle school started, there are classes and family and friends and this thing with my mom and . . . all of it, I guess. It feels like it's all spinning. Do you ever feel that way?"

I felt in my pocket for my mom's letter. "All the time," I said. "Sometimes I feel like I can't keep up."

"The thing is," Austin continued, "I'm happy for my mom—she left for New York yesterday, and she seemed real excited. But if she ends up wanting to go to the cooking school, that means I'll spend almost a year living with only my dad. And that's just weird."

"I know what you mean," I said, because I did. It

wasn't that I loved Mom more than Dad. It's just that he worked so much, it was easier to feel closer to Mom. After she died, it took a while for Dad and me to figure out a pattern with just the two of us. I'd thought we were doing pretty good. Then he met Melanie, and things changed again.

Austin looked over at me. "Yeah," he said slowly. "I guess you *do* know what I mean."

"Do you get along with your dad?" I asked, and I could feel Austin raise his shoulders in a slight shrug.

"Sort of. But he thinks I'm lazy and I play too many video games—and that if I want to play basketball in my driveway every night, I should try out for the team at school. He's got lots of opinions—and he thinks I should have the same ones. If he starts getting too tough about it, Mom usually says something to him. But she might not be there to do that next year, you know?"

Mom always said Worry was a pesky bee that comes buzzing into your mind, trying to drive you crazy, and that you shouldn't worry until you definitely have something to worry about. But Austin looked like he had a whole hive buzzing through his brain as he stared up at the stars, and I realized I wasn't the only one who had things they wanted to forget tonight.

"It'll be okay," I said to Austin. "Things will work out."

"Thanks, Violet."

We laid in the dark for a while, staring at the sky and listening to each other breathe, until we both felt ready to go home.

CHAPTER 21

THE PERFECT FAMILY OF FOUR

As soon as we got back to Austin's house, I grabbed my backpack from the garage and checked my phone. There were five voice mails from Dad and one text, all in caps: COME HOME NOW!

"Someone's busted," Austin said, reading over my shoulder. "What did you do?"

"I don't know." I glanced at the clock, and suddenly, I remembered. "I'm late! Melanie wanted me home earlier."

I blasted out of Austin's house and hurried back home as fast as I could. When I rounded the corner on my street, I came to a dead stop. Dad had decorated the outside of the house—the first time he'd bothered in a couple of years.

Pastel-hued twinkle lights lined the roof and windows. With the brown paint and thick white trim, it looked like a gingerbread house. Nearly all the windows were lit with buttery yellow light, like the house was issuing an invitation, saying, *"It's okay. Come on in. Come home."* I walked slowly down the rest of the street and caught the scent of sugar cookies wafting from the house. It looked like a house from a movie, and all at once the Terrible Beautiful Ache came back and squeezed so tight that it felt like I couldn't breathe.

A Christmas tree with sparkling white lights stood front and center in the downstairs bay window. Dad, Melanie, Joey, and Olivia were clustered around it, hanging ornaments. I saw a couple that I recognized: the snowman I'd made in first grade; the "Baby's First Christmas" ornament Mom had given to Dad the year I was born. But that was it—all the others must have belonged to Melanie.

As I watched, Dad lifted Joey, who plopped a golden star on the top branch of the tree, while Melanie and Olivia cheered. They looked like a Christmas card. Like the perfect family of four.

But I knew, as soon as I stepped inside and entered the picture, I'd ruin it all.

CHAPTER 22

OPEN UP
THE UGLY

Silently, I let myself into the house. I could hear talking and laughing and Joey's high-pitched squeals as Dad tickled him. All of it vanished as soon as Joey caught sight of me, and said, "Violet, look at the tree!"

Dad, Melanie, and Olivia fell silent.

"You decorated the tree without me?" I said, and my voice sounded hoarse.

"You didn't give us much choice, did you?" From the flinty look in Dad's eyes, I knew he was angry. Angrier than I'd seen him since right after Mom died. "Where *were* you?" he demanded. "And why is there mud all over your clothes?"

Melanie grabbed his arm. "Mitch—not now. It's clear Violet's upset—"

"Yes, *now*." Mitch shook her off. "Violet—this is unacceptable. Melanie *told* you to come home early."

"Mitch, I didn't actually tell her what time—"

"I don't care what you did or did not tell her." To me, he said, "She told you to come home early. It's a simple request, and for once, you could've honored it."

"I meant to," I said. "I just got busy. I was at Austin's and lost track of time."

"I know I've given you a wide leash—"

"A *wide leash*? I'm not a *dog*, Dad."

"And that's my fault. I should have been more present this last year. But there are going to be some changes around here. We're trying to build a family and a home—"

"But it's not my family! And it's definitely not my home!" I knew I should shut up and stop right there, but I'd spent so much time *not* saying anything, my words had built up, full as a toxic lake, and it was like someone had thrown the floodgates wide open and all the ugly inside me was spewing out. "This is Melanie's home, and Joey and Olivia's. But it's not mine! You never asked me if I wanted to move to a new house or if I wanted the Hammer for a stepmother—"

"Don't you dare call her—"

"Or Joey or Olivia for siblings. You never asked—but I don't! I don't want to be a family, okay? I liked things the way they were before you had to ruin it by getting married again!"

When I finally stopped to take a breath, Joey was crying. Both Melanie and Olivia looked like I'd slapped them. And worst of all, Dad was staring at me like I was someone he didn't recognize. Or maybe like someone he *did* recognize, but didn't like all that much.

"Melanie, can you take Joey and Olivia upstairs?" Dad said quietly. "I'd like to talk to my daughter alone."

Once they were gone, the anger seemed to deflate from him, and he said, "I'm sorry this is so hard for you. I'm sorry you're so unhappy. But is it really so terrible living here?"

His eyes were wide and filled to the brim with a Terrible Beautiful Ache of his own. I saw a flash of Crying Dad, and I didn't want him to come back. Crying Dad would spend the whole weekend in his bed and never remember to do things like buy new milk or take the trash out. It had been scary, living with Crying Dad.

I swallowed hard. "No. It's not terrible . . . but it's not all that great, either," I added, because Dad always wants me to Talk About It; but how can I really talk to him if I can never tell him the truth? If I'm always scared that Crying Dad will come back?

"It feels like their family is more important than our family," I continued.

"But that's just the thing, Champ," he said softly. "There's not *their* family and *our* family. There's the five of us, together. But that will never start to feel normal unless you decide to accept it. You've got to *try*, Violet."

"I *am* trying," I said.

"No"—he shook his head sadly—"you're really not."

CHAPTER
23

IN THE
DOGHOUSE

Dear Mom,

*Remember how when you would get mad at Dad you'd
give him your I'm Really Annoyed With You look, then
he'd place his hand over his heart, and say, "Oh, no,
Lovely Kate—I'm in your doghouse tonight!" Then he'd
start barking, and you'd start laughing, and it was like
you weren't mad at him anymore.*

*Well, I'm in the doghouse right now with everyone,
and a stupid joke isn't going to make it better. Even if
I wanted to tell a joke to Melanie, I can't, because after*

last night I'm not sure she'll ever speak to me again. And I don't know if Olivia or Joey will, either.

You know how I've been trying really hard not to say all the nasty words inside of me? Well, it's kind of like when you shake up a can of soda and then pop it open: All my nasty words just sprayed all over everyone last night and left a big mess that I don't know how to clean up.

I had an appointment with Coco Martin today, and when I told her what had happened, she said that at least I was finally telling people how I really feel, and that was progress. I'm not so sure. I think a lot of people are only interested in how you're really feeling when how you're really feeling is good. But maybe that's just me.

I didn't tell Izzy, Sophia, and Daisy about the fight at lunch today. I tried, but I just couldn't get the words out. I don't know why, but sometimes I feel like their problems are really small. I know that's not fair to say, but that's honestly how I feel.

See? There are just so many nasty things inside me.

Coco says it's good to find people you can be honest with. I'm glad I can be honest with you, and I still like to believe that you can see me and see this letter. There are so many things I wish I could ask you about. For instance, Boys. How do you know for sure if a boy likes you? Last night Austin was close enough to me that he could smell my lip gloss, which felt really weird. And also a little wondrous. (I put "wondrous" at the top of my list of Words I Love, because it's my favorite one right now.) I'm pretty sure I like Austin and that he likes me back. I haven't told Izzy, Sophia, and Daisy yet, but I'm going to tomorrow night when I spend the night at Izzy's house. Sometimes I look at pictures of you and Dad and wonder what you thought the first time you laid eyes on him, or how you knew he was the One. I never thought to ask you, and sometimes it makes me so mad that I'll never get to ask, ever.

Love always,
Violet

CHAPTER
24

AN INVITATION
TO STAY

The only thing lonelier than being alone is being alone in a house full of people who don't want to talk to you. When we first moved in a couple weeks ago, everyone was tiptoeing around each other. Now everyone just tiptoes around *me*.

"Olivia?" I knocked on her door. "Are you in there?"

It was Friday night, two nights after I'd gone sledding with Austin, and mostly everyone in the house was ignoring me. At school earlier today, Melanie and I almost collided in the halls, until she spun abruptly on her heel and walked away.

"Olivia?" I knocked again. "Can I talk to you?"

I needed to get moving if I wanted to get to the sleepover at Izzy's on time, but I wanted to apologize to Olivia first. I'd tried to today in the cafeteria, but she ran away from me so fast, you'd think I had a disease. Which maybe I did: jerkitis.

"Come on, Olivia," I called. "I know you're in there. Your light is on."

Still no answer, but Olivia's iPod began blasting at full volume.

"Fine! Message received!" I yelled, but I doubt she heard me. I headed downstairs to say good-bye to Dad. He was in the kitchen with Melanie, slicing bell peppers while she unloaded groceries. *Remember to try*, I told myself, and I went to help her unload. "So, Melanie, what are you guys doing tonight?" I asked, all casual, as I stuck bundles of pasta into the pantry.

Melanie shrugged noncommittally and stepped around me to put away the milk. "Nothing much," she said.

"Really, you didn't plan anything?" I asked, but Melanie just shrugged again and kept unloading bags.

Dad, who had stopped slicing to watch us, said, "I think we're going to make pizza and watch Christmas movies."

"That sounds nice," I said. It sounded really nice, actually, and I remembered "Watch Christmas movies" was on Mom's list. Even though I was about to leave for the sleepover, I almost wished they would invite me to stay and eat dinner with them.

Because after what I'd said the other night, it felt like I needed an invitation.

When an invitation didn't come, I said, "Okay, well, I guess I'll see you guys tomorrow."

"Do you want me to drive you to Izzy's?" Dad asked, wiping his hands on a towel. "It's pretty cold out there tonight."

"No, I'm good," I said, hefting my backpack over my shoulder. "I'd rather walk, and she's got a sleeping bag I can borrow. I'll see you tomorrow. Bye, Melanie," I said.

"Bye," Melanie said shortly, but she didn't look at me.

"Just give her a little time," Dad whispered as we left the kitchen. "Her feelings are hurt, but she'll come around."

"Thanks, Dad," I said. "I feel awful."

"I know you do . . . and I know you have to leave soon, but do you have time for a quick chat?"

"Um, sure," I said, even though I really needed to leave. My stomach twisted into knots. I'd been waiting for him to say something about the fight, and I wondered how much trouble I was in.

"I'm sorry," I said as soon as we sat down on the couch in the living room. "I know I was a big jerk the other night."

Dad didn't disagree with me. "Well . . . while I didn't care for the manner in which you expressed yourself, I always want to hear how you're feeling." He looked nervous and his words came out slightly stiff, like he'd been practicing them. I couldn't help but wonder if he'd had a chat with Coco Martin and received her "How to Talk to Your Tween Daughter" pep talk, and I actually had to stop myself from smiling. "I want you to feel like you can talk to me," he added.

"Sometimes I feel like I can't," I blurted. The minute the words were out of my mouth, I wanted to take them back. But I knew if things were really going to get better, we needed to start talking. Really talking. I took a deep breath, and said, "After Mom died, you spent a lot of time in your room. You cried a lot, and sometimes it felt scary to be around you. But you've been so happy since you met Melanie, I guess I didn't want to ruin anything for you."

"You couldn't ruin anything for me, Champ," Dad said, looking pained. "I *want* you to talk to me. I always have. And I'm sorry for disappearing for a while like that. I wish I could go back and change that—you have no idea how much. And I'm sorry this month has been so difficult for you." He sighed and ran a hand through his hair. "I don't know, maybe Melanie and I should've had a longer engagement. Gave you kids more time to get used—"

"It's not that," I said. "I guess it's just . . . sometimes I feel like Olivia's friends and Olivia's plans are more important than mine." I thought how to best say it. "It's like, because the things she likes to do—the newspaper, the Eco Club, and the baton-twirling team—are related to school, it's like those things get treated like they're more important than when I want to be with the Charm Girls or just be by myself. And I don't like that."

"I can see that." Dad nodded. "And I know you've been watching Joey a lot after school. Maybe I could—"

"I don't mind watching Joey," I said. "It's been kind of fun, actually. I guess I just wish my charm club was as important as Olivia's clubs."

Dad nodded again. "That makes sense. I don't think Melanie and I realized that." He still looked nervous, like he was worried he'd say or do the wrong thing.

The whole conversation felt strange and awkward. It wasn't that Dad and I had a bad relationship; it was just that since he's always worked so much, it was easier to go to Mom with my problems. Now, a year and a half later after she'd died, we needed to start figuring out our new pattern. I think Dad felt the same way, because he let out a breath, and said, "I guess I'm just not good at all this. . . . Your mother . . ." He stopped and swallowed. "I still really miss her," he finished quietly.

"I know, Dad. I do, too. But," I added, "I'm really glad you have Melanie."

And in that moment, I realized I truly meant it.

CHAPTER 25

SLEEPOVER

"Thank God you're here," Izzy said when she opened her front door. "I need you to settle a fight between Grandma Bertie and Aunt Mildred before they kill each other." She pulled me inside the house, and said, "Are you okay? You look upset."

"I'm fine," I said.

Izzy pursed her lips like she wanted to say something, but led me into the living room, where Grandma Bertie and Aunt Mildred were bickering.

"You cannot go on a date with Scooter wearing your old-lady tennis shoes," Grandma Bertie was saying to Aunt Mildred, who looked ready to throttle her.

"For your information, Bertha, I *am* an old lady. So are you. In fact, since you're nine minutes older than me, you're an even *older* lady."

"Watch who you're calling old. Age is just a state of mind, dear."

"My mistake then. Because if that's true, then you're a bona fide two-year-old."

"And your shoes look like they belong to—" Grandma Bertie stopped abruptly when she caught sight of me. "Hi, Violet."

"Hi, Grandma Bertie. Hi, Aunt Mildred," I said, smiling. After the strained silence in my house, the usual chaos in Izzy's was nice. I decided to try to forget about my fight with Melanie and Olivia. Tonight, I just wanted to enjoy the sleepover. Grandma Bertie and Aunt Mildred were standing in front of the Malone's big Christmas tree. They'd pulled it out to the center of the room—perfect for sleeping under it tonight and checking "Have a sleepover under a Christmas tree" off Mom's list.

"What do you think, Violet?" Izzy asked. "Do you think the shoes are okay?"

"Yeah, do you?" Aunt Mildred said. "And before you answer, just remember who buys those lovely charms hanging from that bracelet you're wearing."

I thought about how when Austin and I were walking home from ice-blocking, he said that next time we went, I should wear old clothes in case we ended up in the mud again.

"I think the shoes are fine," I said. "If he really likes you, he won't care what you wear."

"I *told* you," Aunt Mildred said to Grandma Bertie. "So stop trying to boss me around."

The doorbell rang, and Izzy and I went to answer it. Sophia struggled inside, carrying two big bags.

"Geez, what do you have in here?" Izzy asked, taking one of them from her. "You're just staying one night."

"It's not clothes," Sophia answered. "It's all my mom's Christmas movies—for your mom's list," she told me. "And we have to watch at least two, because it said, 'Watch Christmas Movies,' plural. So we can't just watch one."

"What's in the other bag?" Izzy asked.

"Baking supplies." Sophia dropped it in the hallway, and it landed on the ground with a loud *thunk*.

Scooter McGee arrived next and handed Aunt Mildred a bouquet of roses. "Beautiful flowers, for a beautiful lady," he said. "Hello, girls," he added, turning to us. "I hear there's a sleepover in the works tonight."

"Yep," Izzy answered. "Where are you taking Aunt Mildred tonight?"

"I thought we'd take a stroll around Dandelion Square. Lovely shoes, by the way, Milly. Very sensible," he said, and Aunt Mildred shot Grandma Bertie a triumphant look.

"You've been taking Aunt Mildred on a lot of dates," Izzy said. "Is she your girlfriend now?"

"Izzy, dear," Grandma Bertie said quickly, "your mouth is getting ahead of itself again."

"I am entirely too old to be having boyfriends," Aunt Mildred said. "Now get these bags out of the hallway, before someone trips and breaks an arm."

"I rather like the word 'boyfriend,'" Scooter was saying as they left and he shut the door behind him.

"Do you think Aunt Mildred and Scooter are boyfriend and girlfriend?" Sophia asked me. "Like, do you think they've actually kissed?"

"I don't know. I haven't really thought about it," I said, which was sort of a lie, because I had thought about it. Or at least, I wondered about that kind of stuff all the time. I wondered what it was like to have a crush on a boy and have him like you back enough to become boyfriend and girlfriend. And how do you decide that a boy isn't just a boyfriend, but the One?

All this talk about boyfriends and girlfriends was making me want to tell the Charm Girls about my crush on Austin. But there wasn't much time to talk about boys and crushes because the doorbell rang again just a minute later. It was a delivery guy, who handed over four large pizzas just as Daisy arrived. After we ate, Sophia insisted we watch Christmas movies while we made the gingerbread houses to earn our charm. Once the houses were sitting in the kitchen, Sophia pulled out her supplies so we could bake Christmas cookies. After that, she made us sing carols, which was pretty funny, since all four of us have bad voices, but Sophia said at least we could check it off Mom's list.

When it was getting later and everyone was starting to yawn, we rolled out our sleeping bags under the Christmas tree.

"Does everyone have their charm?" Izzy asked.

Once we were all holding them, she said, "We have earned our charms," and we all hooked the tiny gingerbread houses to our bracelets. Once I finished, I put it on and shook my wrist. I noticed that the more charms I put on it, the more noise it made when I moved. Now when the charms clinked together, it made a musical sound. Almost like jingle bells.

"Let's play Truth or Dare!" Daisy said.

"But that's not on Violet's mom's list," Sophia protested.

Everyone turned to me, and I said, "That's okay; I'd love to play Truth or Dare."

I figured I'd just pick Truth and hope that someone would ask me if I liked anyone, so I could tell everyone about my crush on Austin. I was pretty sure I was even going to call crush dibs on him.

"All right, let's do it," Daisy said. "I'll go first. I pick Dare!"

"Okay." Izzy thought about it for a second. "I dare you to run around outside barefoot!"

"Are you crazy?" I said. "It's freezing out there." But Daisy had already ripped off her socks and was running for the door. Even though she was out there for only a minute, by the time she came back, her lips looked slightly bluish. "I can't feel my fingers," she said through chattering teeth. She dove back into her sleeping bag.

Sophia went next, and she picked Truth. "What are you most scared of?" Daisy asked her.

Sophia didn't even have to think about it. "That my parents will get divorced," she answered. Mr. and Mrs. Ramos are separated—Mr. Ramos stayed in San Francisco while the rest of Sophia's family moved to Dandelion

Hollow last summer. Sophia had said it without hesitation. And even though she said she was afraid, she didn't look afraid. Her eyes were wide and clear, like she was ready to face the truth head-on, whatever it was. I wondered if I ever looked that brave when I was scared.

If Izzy had asked me right then what I was most scared of, I would have said I was afraid that right now, at this very minute, Dad, Melanie, Joey, and Olivia were all sprawled out in the living room watching Christmas movies. Laughing, having a good time, and not missing me at all. Happier without me.

"I'm sure they'll be okay," I said quietly. I didn't know if that was true, but I do know that when people are worried, sometimes it's just best to say hopeful things to them.

"Thanks, Violet," Sophia said.

"It's my turn!" Izzy said. "I pick Truth!"

"Okay." Sophia perked up as she thought of a question. "Do you still like Austin Jackson?" she asked.

I tried not to roll my eyes. This question again? Izzy had already answered it. Besides, I wanted someone to ask *me* who I liked.

"Well . . . ," Izzy said slowly. "I don't know."

Wait, *what*? I sat up in my sleeping bag. What did she just say?

"What do you mean, you don't know?" I said. "How can you not know if you like him? Either you like him—or you don't. It's that simple."

"It's not that simple, Violet," Sophia said, shooting me a strange look.

"Well, I don't understand," I said to Izzy. "You've been telling us all month you don't like him. Now all of a sudden you're not sure?"

"I haven't been saying that," Izzy said. "When have I been saying that? I said it, like, once."

"So . . . do you?" Sophia asked.

"She just said she doesn't like him," I said.

"No, *you* said she doesn't like him," Daisy said, sounding annoyed. "So back off and let her answer the question."

"Yeah, Violet," Izzy said. "Stop being so bossy."

"Sorry," I mumbled.

"So . . . do you like him?" Sophia persisted.

"I'm not sure," Izzy said. "But . . . has anyone noticed how cute he's gotten the last month?"

Daisy and Sophia both nodded, and I wanted to scream. "There's more to liking a boy than just thinking he's cute," I said, and the three of them shot me irritated looks again, and I knew I'd better cool it. But I also knew I was right. I mean, sure, I had liked other boys because they were cute. But it was different with Austin. I liked him because we could really talk to each other about the things that mattered. I could text him at midnight if I wanted, and he'd be there to answer me back. Plus, I was pretty sure I was a lot closer to Austin than Izzy was. I was the girl he could talk to about his mom and the cooking school she might go to, and Izzy was . . . his next-door neighbor and the girl he sometimes played basketball with. There was a big difference.

"I think maybe I'm changing my mind," Izzy said. Her face brightened. "In fact, I think I've definitely changed my mind. I like him. I re-crush dibs him!"

Re-crush dibs?

I flopped back onto my sleeping bag. This was *not* how tonight was supposed to go. I was supposed to feel like one of them. I was supposed to feel like a normal middle schooler chatting with her friends about the boy she likes. Instead, I felt two seconds away from hollering at Izzy. And worst of all, I felt like a rotten friend for liking my best friend's crush.

"Violet, it's your turn," Daisy said. "Truth or Dare?"

"Dare," I said miserably. Because I didn't want to lie if they asked me who I liked. But I definitely couldn't tell them the truth. Not anymore.

26

WHO'S SMARTER?

Why are the perfect gifts so hard to find?

It was Sunday afternoon, two days after the sleepover, and I still hadn't figured out what to get Izzy for her Secret Santa gift. I still believed the best presents didn't cost any money, but with Christmas only a couple weeks away, I was running out of time. I decided to make a list of Things Izzy Likes:

- STARS
- BOOTS
- SKIRTS
- DONUTS

The list wasn't much help. I couldn't exactly purchase a star for her—they kind of belong to everyone, already— and even though I know Izzy likes thrift shopping, I didn't think she would like someone thrift shopping *for* her. But I really wanted to get her something that would tell her how happy I was that we were friends again—even if we both liked the same boy.

I was still racking my brains for an answer when Austin texted:

What are you doing right now?

Not much. Going to start working on our essay soon.

You're doing it all without me? Sweet!

Ha ha . . . I figured since I'm smarter than you, I might as well.

Hmm . . . you're doing all the work, but we're both going to get the same grade. NOW who's smarter? Work on it later. Come over and we can go ice-blocking.

A part of me really wanted to text him back and tell him I'd be right there. But remembering Izzy's smile on Friday night when she said she liked him stopped me.

Can't. I have lots of homework to do.

So do I, but you don't see that stopping me. Where are your priorities?

Next time.

But I wasn't sure there would be a next time. Izzy

had a crush on Austin first, and that meant I couldn't like him. If your best friend likes someone, and she tells you she likes him, and then you turn around and start liking him, you're the bad guy. That may not make very much sense, but in middle school, that's just the way it is.

I'd been thinking about it all weekend, and I really did like Austin. In some ways, I felt like I could talk to him more than anyone—even Izzy. But I was glad to finally be friends—good friends—with Izzy again, and I wasn't going to let a boy come between us.

I rolled over onto my back and stared at the ceiling. I didn't feel like studying, and I also didn't want to be alone anymore, either.

I picked up my phone again and called Izzy's house phone. The line was busy, so I had to call her on my walkie-talkie: "Wordnerd to Stargazer, do you copy?"

It took a couple tries, but a few minutes later the walkie squawked to life: "I copy, Wordnerd. What's up?"

"Want to hang out? I could come over to your house—" I stopped, because I didn't want to be at Izzy's house, not since she lived right next door to Austin. "Actually, you could come over to my house. You could help me figure out how to decorate my new room."

I stared around at the white walls. I still hadn't hung anything up, and except for my books and clothes, most of my stuff was still in boxes. I guess in a lot of ways, Dad was right: I wasn't trying to make this my home.

"I can't come over," Izzy said, sounding apologetic.

"Why not?"

There was a crackling silence, and at first I thought Izzy had cut out. "Uh . . . I'm sick," she said.

"Okay. Maybe later if you feel better?"

"Um . . . sure. Maybe later. I'll call you."

We said good-bye and I walked downstairs. Melanie, Olivia, and Joey were sitting at the kitchen table, each of them pouring over a list.

"What are you guys doing?"

"Making Christmas lists—I'm taking Joey and Olivia shopping."

Melanie and Olivia wouldn't look at me. I knew they were both still upset about the other night, and I figured if I was going to start making an effort, I needed to start somewhere.

"Can I come?" I asked.

Olivia looked up and glared at me. "Don't you have plans with your friends?"

"Izzy's sick," I answered, just as Melanie said, "Olivia,

knock it off." She smiled tentatively at me. "Really, you want to come?"

"Sure," I replied, remembering what Dad had said about trying harder. "Shopping sounds fun."

Sometimes a person's eyes can say things. In this case, I hoped mine said, *I'm sorry* and *I'm trying*. I think they did, because Melanie nodded, and said, "Of course you can come. Let's pack up and get going."

We drove to Dandelion Square instead of walking, because Melanie didn't want everyone carrying a bunch of bags home. I rode in the back with Joey.

"Mom gave me some money to buy Dad a present," he said.

It took me a second to realize that Joey meant my dad, and not Mr. Vanderberg.

"I thought you already gave him a present?" I said.

"Yeah, but I want to get him another one."

"Really? What are you going to get him?"

"I don't know." Joey frowned. "I can't think of anything."

"I have some ideas," I said. "Do you want me to show you a few things he likes?"

Joey nodded happily, and I caught Melanie staring at me in the rearview mirror. As soon as our eyes met, she glanced away quickly. But I was pretty sure her eyes had been saying *thank you*.

Sometimes you can say a lot without saying anything at all.

After we found a parking space, we went to Barnaby's Antiques to say hi to Dad. He was busy with customers, so he could only wave at us. After that, we went to Charming Trinkets to pick up a pair of earrings for Emily, Olivia's friend from her baton-twirling team. I was hoping we'd see Sophia or her mom, but we didn't. Our next stop was the olive-oil shop so Melanie could get some presents for a couple of teachers at Dandelion Middle. As she finished ringing up her purchases, Joey tugged at my shirt.

"Where should we find a present for Dad?"

I caught Melanie staring at me, waiting for me to answer. This time, I was pretty sure her eyes were saying, *I know this is hard, but please be nice to him.*

"Harrison's Hardware," I answered. "There are lots of things he likes there."

Harrison's Hardware is brightly lit with wooden floors strewn with sawdust and aisles that seem to go on forever. They sell a lot more than just hardware items. Everything from wrenches to model airplanes to kitchen gadgets to candles and Christmas decorations. The back of the store is Dad's favorite, because that's where they sell penny candy.

"His favorites are the butterscotches and the Christmas-ribbon candy," I told Joey once I'd led everyone to the candy bins.

Joey counted out the change in his pocket and frowned. "I guess I could get him butterscotches this year, and ribbon candy next year," he said.

Next year.

Those two words nearly knocked me sideways. I think some part of me had been hoping that our new living arrangement—the five of us together—was temporary. But it wasn't. Next year Melanie might take us all Christmas shopping again. And the year after that and the year after that—it could be another new pattern, like Mom talked about in her letter.

While Joey was counting out butterscotches and putting them into a plastic bag, we heard a voice from the next aisle over. It belonged to Edith Binchy: "What Mitch Barnaby sees in her, I'll *never* understand."

At that, Melanie, Olivia, and I all froze. Edith couldn't see us from where we stood, but I peeked quickly around the aisle and saw her. She was standing in front of a candle display talking to a couple of the Knattering Knitters, who were nodding at her enthusiastically.

"Melanie Harmer had her sights set on that man from the moment she met him," Edith continued.

That was a total lie. I know, because I was actually there the moment Dad and Melanie met. It was a bright, windy day in early June, and Dad and I were taking a tour of Dandelion Middle. Melanie had been crying—over Mr. Vanderberg not remembering to call Joey on his birthday, we found out later. She'd been so upset that she'd bumped right into Dad, and the English essays in her hands went flying into the wind, swirling like a paper snowstorm.

"I'm so sorry!" she'd said as she grabbed wildly at the essays.

"It's no problem," Dad had said, and they both crouched down to pick up the ones that had landed on the cement. "We all have bad days sometimes."

Melanie had given a half-laugh. "Ever feel like you're having a bad year?"

Melanie wasn't even looking at Dad as she straightened up the essays. But he was looking at her. "All the time," he'd said softly.

I remembered that on that day I thought Melanie seemed nice, and I hoped she'd be my English teacher. Of course, that was before Dad had asked her out a month later when they'd bumped into each other again at Don's Donuts; before they started spending a ton of time together, before the night they made me, Olivia, and Joey meet one another and told us they were Officially Dating.

Edith Binchy didn't know any of that, and she was flapping her mouth all over town, anyway. I think Melanie could tell I was mad, because she laid a hand on my arm, and said, "Violet, just let it go. It's not worth it."

"What do you mean? She's totally lying, you know she is."

"I know, but some people you just can't reason with. And if you go over there, she'll be sure to tell the whole town how you accosted her when she was just innocently minding her own business."

"It's okay, Violet, really—we're used to it," Olivia added, and I noticed for the first time that she chewed on her cheek, just like Melanie does sometimes.

"Used to it? Does stuff like this happen a lot?" I asked.

Melanie and Olivia glanced at each other uneasily. "A lot of people in this town really loved your mom," Melanie said finally. "It's best to just let it go."

Grudgingly, I followed them up to the cash register so Joey could pay for the candy. I didn't understand why people were so upset with Melanie just because they liked Mom. It wasn't Melanie's fault Mom had gotten sick and died—even *I* knew that.

We were all quiet as we left the store. "Do you guys want to get a slice of pie from the Kaleidoscope?" Melanie said, and I could tell she was trying to cheer us up.

"Yes!" Joey said. "A big one with lots of whipped cream!"

We walked into the café and Melanie told us to find a seat while she ordered from the counter. We slid into a circular booth near the back. I checked my phone; Austin had sent me a text:

Are you finished studying yet? I'm bored. You know you want to hang out with me. We could cross something off your mom's list.

I was debating whether or not to respond when Olivia suddenly said, "Aren't those your friends?"

I looked over. Sophia and Izzy were walking across Dandelion Square, their moms following behind them. Sophia, Mrs. Malone, and Mrs. Ramos stopped to admire the town Christmas tree, while Izzy kept moving forward, heading straight for the café.

"Didn't you say you couldn't hang out with Izzy today

because she's sick?" Olivia asked. "She doesn't look that sick to me."

"She doesn't," I agreed.

In fact, Izzy looked better than ever. Instead of her usual tie-dyed skirt and combat boots, she was dressed up in a red-velvet dress. All four of them were dressed up, actually.

Olivia stared at me curiously. "So . . . what are you going to do?"

"I don't know. Maybe it's nothing. Maybe there's a really good explanation."

But from the way Izzy's expression whitened when she walked into the café and saw Olivia and me, I doubted it.

"I'm going to talk to her," I said.

Olivia nodded. "Good idea."

"It's not what you think," Izzy said as soon as I approached.

"Oh yeah?" I crossed my arms. "What am I thinking?" When she didn't immediately answer, I said, "You look great—you must have gotten a lot better real fast."

"Okay, okay." She puffed out a breath. "I'm not sick."

"Shocker," I said. "So why did you say you were? If you had plans with Sophia, you could have just told me."

"Because . . ." Izzy sighed. "Because it's a

mother-daughter thing. Mrs. Ramos and my mom got tickets to this stupid play—the one I told you about, remember?—and they are *making* me go. And I didn't want to tell you about it because—"

Izzy was known for sticking her foot in her mouth, but this time she stopped herself. It didn't matter, though, because I knew what she was going to say. The elephant in the room, the thing I never wanted to talk about, because it couldn't ever be made better: I didn't have a mother, so I couldn't do things like have a mother-daughter date with my best friend. All I had was Melanie, who let me crash *her* mother-daughter date with Olivia. And even if we could read each other's eyes, it still wasn't the same.

My phone pinged again. I was pretty sure it was Austin. And suddenly, I couldn't remember why I didn't want to hang out with him today.

Izzy was pulling nervously at her dress. "Violet, can we talk—"

"Forget it," I said, flipping over my phone to text Austin. "Have fun at the play."

If Izzy could lie to me so she could spend time on a mother-daughter date, I could hang out with Austin and cross a few more items off Mom's list. Because with her gone, that list was the only thing I had left of her.

27

HURT FEELINGS

Dear Mom,

My ugly came spilling out again. I got really mad at Izzy
a couple days ago. She lied to me about going to a play
with Sophia and their moms on a mother-daughter date.
I know she did it only because she didn't want to hurt
my feelings. But it made me mad anyway, and when she
tried calling me later that night on the walkie-talkie, I
turned it off without saying anything to her.

Then this afternoon, Aunt Mildred asked us all to
meet at the Kaleidoscope Café so she could give us

another round of charms. As soon as Izzy arrived
she started apologizing, and I finally just said that
everything was fine.

But everything definitely isn't fine. I'm not mad at her
anymore, but I know I need to tell her that I have a crush
on Austin. Especially since Austin and I hung out last
night, listening to some of your old records so we could
cross it off your list. We met up at Barnaby's Antiques,
and Dad let us listen to the records in an alcove off the
shop while we worked on our Egyptian essay. (Okay,
while I worked on the essay—Austin mostly wandered
around the shop looking to see if Dad had any old comic
books for sale.)

When he'd finally finished his search, we listened to
Louis Armstrong and Ella Fitzgerald, and I couldn't
help tearing up a little. When he asked me what was
wrong, I told him they were your favorite musicians. He
didn't make fun of me or think I was a baby. He just
asked how many items I still had left to check off. When
I pulled out the list and showed him, he said he had an
idea for how we could check something else off. I keep
wondering what it is.

I'm still enjoying the Charm Club. Aunt Mildred gave us a tiny Christmas present charm and asked us to volunteer for Dandelion Hollow's annual Wrap-a-Thon. She said she was inspired by your list, so that's something else I can check off soon. I'm pretty sure I can finish most of it before Christmas. Not all of it, though. I don't see how I'll be able to cross off "Make a snow angel," unless Dad takes me somewhere where it actually snows. I'm working on it, though.

Love always,
Violet

28

ROASTING
MARSHMALLOWS

"Hey, Melanie?" I said as I stepped into the kitchen. "Austin just texted me. Can I walk over to his house right now?"

Melanie made a check mark on the paper she was grading. "Are you two working on your project again?"

I considered telling her yes, but decided against it. "Well, no. He said he has an idea for something I could check off Mom's list." I figured by now Olivia had told her about Mom's list.

I'm pretty sure I was right, because Melanie nodded like she knew exactly what I was talking about. "Sure," she said, and looked up hopefully. "Why don't you take Olivia with you? She's upstairs in her room."

Remember to try, I repeated to myself. "Um, okay," I said.

"Come in!" Olivia said after I knocked on her bedroom door. She was sitting cross-legged on her bed, doing homework.

"Austin invited me over to roast marshmallows at his house," I said. "Do you want to come? I thought it would be fun if we went together."

Olivia gave me a look as if to say, *Yeah, right*. "You mean, *my mom* thought it would be fun if we went together, right?" she said.

"No," I said quickly, and Olivia cocked her head. "Okay, fine. Yeah, she did."

Olivia smirked and went back to her homework. "Maybe next time." She glanced back up. "But have fun, okay?"

By the time I'd arrived at the Jacksons, Austin and his dad had already set up a portable fire pit in their front yard. "Ready to roast some marshmallows?" Austin asked as Mr. Jackson lit the fire.

"Definitely," I said.

"That should be good for a while," Mr. Jackson said as the fire roared to life. "Holler if you need anything," he added, before going back inside the house.

"What's it been like, being by yourself with your dad?" I asked as I took the marshmallow and roasting stick Austin offered.

"All right." Austin shrugged and made a face. "Except he told me I was going to have to make dinner a couple times a week."

"Poor you," I teased. "You'll have to actually start taking care of yourself for a change."

"Nah." Austin grinned. "I'm just going to let you keep making me soup."

"Yeah, I'll get right on that," I said, and we both laughed.

We got quiet after that, and stared at the fire—until we heard the bounce of a ball behind us, followed by Izzy's voice saying, "What are you guys doing out here?"

"Roasting marshmallows," Austin said. "Want one?"

"Sure," Izzy plunked down next to me. "Want to play basketball afterward?"

"Nah," Austin said. "I'm good."

Austin went to get a new bag of marshmallows. While he was gone, Izzy said, "He's still acting weird. He didn't want to play basketball last night, either."

I stared into the fire, watching the flames lick at the marshmallow I was roasting, and didn't answer her. Last night Austin and I had been texting back and forth about a mystery we'd both been watching on TV. Between the two of us, we figured out who'd done it.

"So," Izzy began, and even though I wasn't looking at her, I could hear the frown in her voice. "You and Austin hang out sometimes?"

I figured now was the time to tell her about my crush, but just as I opened my mouth, Austin appeared, holding a big bag of marshmallows. "Here you go," he said, handing one to Izzy.

"Geez, you think you have enough?" I asked, because it wasn't like Izzy and I could talk about Austin right in front of his face.

"I don't know, do I?" Austin tossed a marshmallow at me while Izzy toasted hers.

"Careful," Izzy said. "You do that again, and Violet and I might come after you." Her voice held a singsong quality. Was she trying to flirt with Austin?

If so, Austin didn't seem to notice. "I'm not worried." He tossed another marshmallow at me.

"You should be," Izzy said. "I'm a great shot."

"Maybe—but Violet's a lousy shot." He lobbed a third one at me, and it lodged in my hair.

That was it; I'd had enough.

I grabbed the bag from Austin; it split and a ton of marshmallows dropped to the ground. I threw one at him—it missed wildly—then I went running into the street as he started to chase me.

"Get him, Violet!" Izzy called. Like Austin, she'd picked up some marshmallows and was running after us.

"Incoming!" Austin shouted, a split second before a marshmallow struck me on the shoulder.

"You're gonna pay for that!" I yelled, and tossed one at him. It missed completely.

Austin grinned and began to juggle a few marshmallows. "Sure, I am."

Izzy was a much better shot than I was; I kept missing, but she lobbed a few marshmallows that hit Austin in the back. "What's wrong with you?" she shouted at him after another couple hits went unanswered. "Why won't you fight back? What are you, chicken?" she added, but Austin didn't seem to notice. He kept coming at me, missing every time.

"You're not such a great shot now, are you?" I taunted.

"Hey, Austin, eat *this*!" Izzy lobbed a marshmallow right in Austin's face. It was a direct hit—but Austin still kept aiming for me, and missing. I may not be a good shot, but I'm an excellent dodger.

(Total side note: Dodgeball is the only game in PE that I'm ever any good at—because I know how to get out of people's way.)

"It's a good thing you don't play baseball," I called. "Because your aim stinks!"

"*My* aim is great," Izzy said as she launched another assault at Austin.

"*Violet!*" I heard Olivia's voice call from the sidewalk. "*Your dad asked me to come get you. It's time for dinner!*" I glanced over at her, which gave Austin his chance. He threw another one, and it hit me right in the eyeball.

"Ouch!" I yelped.

"I'm sorry, Violet." Austin hurried over. "I guess I'm a more excellent shot than I thought!"

"Excellent," I repeated, blinking rapidly, "as long as your target isn't moving."

He grinned. "At least you can cross roasting marshmallows off your Mom's list."

"Whatever, Austin," I said as I turned to leave with Olivia. To Izzy, I said, "I'll try to call you on the walkie later, okay?"

"Okay," Izzy replied. There was an unreadable expression on her face. And a forgotten marshmallow in her hand.

CHAPTER 29

CANDY CONTRABAND

Later that night after dinner, I was in the kitchen working on my Egyptian essay. Austin and I were pretty far behind, and I couldn't keep waiting for him to finally decide he felt like helping. We still hadn't talked at all about the pyramid model, either. I'd just started making a list of all the materials we needed to buy when Olivia came stomping into the room.

"Are M&M out in the living room?" she asked.

I blinked. "M&M?"

"Mom and Mitch."

"Oh." I thought it was weird she had a nickname for Dad. And not just Dad, but both him and Melanie together, like they were a unit. Which, I guessed, they were. I decided not to think about it. "No, they went upstairs a few minutes ago."

"Awesome." From the back of the pantry Olivia produced a crumpled brown bag. She plunked down next to me and dumped the contents onto the table: chocolate bars, packs of strawberry licorice, butterscotches, Christmas-ribbon candy, and a plastic baggie of cinnamon bears.

"What's all this?" I asked.

"My secret stash from Harrison's Hardware," she said, biting the head off a cinnamon bear. "I need sugar. Want some? Candy is vegetarian, right?"

I glanced out to the hallway as I took a couple licorice whips, just to make sure no one was coming. Not only does Melanie not allow doughnuts and soda at breakfast, she hardly allows any junk food in the house—ever. For dinner, she'd made us this ultrahealthy stir-fry with kale. It was vegetarian and I appreciated it, but still, it was totally gross. Just because I'm a vegetarian doesn't mean I want to spend my life eating yucky green plants.

While I chewed a licorice whip, Olivia angrily ripped open a chocolate bar and inhaled it in a couple bites. She went to eat another one, but when the package wouldn't open, she threw it against the wall, where it split in two.

"Are you okay?" I asked.

In answer, she slid a Christmas card across the table. It was a picture of a family: a couple with a little boy—who looked about two—cuddled between them. They were all wearing the same thick red-and-green sweater and blue jeans in front of a Christmas tree. "That's my dad, Charlie, and Big-Hair Barbie," she said.

"Wow," I said. "She really *does* have big hair." *Big lips, too*, I thought, picking up the card and examining it. Those couldn't be natural. Besides the matching sweaters and jeans, if you looked closely, you could see all three of them were wearing the same Christmas-tree pin. Mr. Vanderberg and Big-Hair Barbie each had an arm around Charlie, their heads tilted toward him, like he was the center of their gravity. There was no mistaking it: Charlie looked coddled and well cared for. Well loved. And Mr. Vanderberg looked like a happy, doting father—not at all like the man who rarely spoke to Joey and Olivia.

"Has Joey seen this?" I asked, giving the card back to Olivia.

"No—and he's not going to." She stared hard at me. "Okay?"

I held up my hands. "I won't say anything, I promise."

Olivia relaxed and shoved a licorice whip into her

mouth. "It's a stupid picture," she said in between angry bites. "I mean, those sweaters are totally tacky."

"They totally are," I agreed.

We ate quietly for a few moments, and I added more items to my pyramid list until Olivia suddenly said, "You know, sometimes I wish he was dead." I looked up, startled, as she made a sound that was a cross between a snort and a sob. "You think I'm evil for saying that, don't you?"

"Umm . . ." I wasn't sure what to say. Truthfully, I couldn't imagine ever wishing something so terrible on anyone.

"It's just that if he was dead," she went on, "then he couldn't help it, you know? It wouldn't be his fault."

I guessed I never thought about it like that. Mom never had a choice; cancer took her away from Dad and me, and in the end, there was nothing any of us could do to stop it. But Mr. Vanderberg *had* a choice. And he chose to leave. I thought maybe I was starting to understand why Olivia was always so willing to help Dad out all the time. Maybe she wasn't trying to replace me, after all. Maybe she was just hoping he'd turn out to be a dad who'd choose to stay.

We were both quiet for a while, and it was nice, sitting in the kitchen, eating Olivia's contraband candy. Sometimes, when I watch a movie and see brothers and

sisters hanging out at home together, I get a funny feeling in my stomach—an empty one, like I've forgotten
to eat dinner. I didn't feel that way now. I felt full, and
not just of licorice—but of something else. Something
warm and good.

"What's going on with you and Austin?" Olivia asked
suddenly.

"What? Nothing's going on," I said, and she rolled her
eyes.

"Um, hello? I have eyes—I was watching you for a bit
during your marshmallow fight. You guys were totally
flirting."

I shrugged. "So what if we were? What's the big deal?"

"It's not—not to *me*, anyway. But Izzy was watching
you two pretty closely."

A knot formed in my stomach. "She was?"

Olivia nodded. "Yeah—and she didn't look too happy.
So do you like him?"

I stared at Olivia, wondering how much I could tell
her. "Yeah, I like him," I said finally.

"And Izzy likes him, too?" she guessed.

"Yeah, but she liked him first."

"Oh," Olivia said, nodding. "So you're the bad guy."

"Yeah, I'm the bad guy. I didn't *mean* to start liking

him. We're doing a class project together, and he's the first boy I've ever felt like I could really talk to."

"Really?" She looked genuinely curious. "What do you talk about?"

"Family, school, deep stuff—the stuff I don't talk about with anyone. Like I can't wait to see him in history class, and sometimes during the day, something will happen to me and I'll think to myself, *I should tell Austin about that.*"

"Wow—I don't know that there's ever been a guy I could talk to like that." She made a face. "Most of the guys at school won't come near me because of my mom."

Now I was the one who was curious. "Is it really hard, having your mom be, well, the Hammer?"

"Yeah," she said as she twisted a licorice whip around her finger. "I can barely walk down the halls without someone hassling me about it." She glanced at me. "I'm sorry my mom keeps trying to make us hang out . . . I mean, I know she wants us to be friends, but I think she thinks she's helping me out at school."

"Has it been difficult making friends this year?" I asked.

Olivia nodded. "Yeah, but it's getting easier." She took a deep breath. "I actually talked to Aunt Mildred—I'm going to buy a charm bracelet and start collecting charms, too."

"You're joining the Charm Girls?" I asked, and I was

surprised to realize the idea didn't bother me the way it would have a month ago.

"No." Olivia shook her head vigorously. "Sorry—that's not what I meant. I'm going to start a charm-bracelet club with Emily and some girls from our math class." She shrugged. "It seems like you, Izzy, Daisy, and Sophia have so much fun—I guess I just thought maybe it would be fun for us, too."

"I think that's a great idea, Olivia."

We ate in silence, until Olivia suddenly said, "There is one huge upside to being related to the Hammer, though."

"There is?" I said. "What is it?"

A huge smile spread across her face. "We'll never have to be in her class!"

We both laughed, and I reached for another licorice whip. As I did, I looked at my bracelet and wondered—since Olivia would soon have her own—if someday we'd have matching charms.

And that gave me an idea.

CHAPTER
30

THE
WRAP-A-THON

The Wrap-a-Thon was being held in Hollow Hall, a multi-purpose building across from Dandelion Square. Aunt Mildred had signed Izzy, Sophia, Daisy, and me up to work the last shift on Friday night. After a dinner of pasta and garlic bread (and a quick dip into Olivia's candy stash when Dad and Melanie weren't looking), Melanie and Olivia dropped me off; they were going out for another round of Christmas shopping.

"Text me if you need anything," Melanie said as she pulled her minivan up to the curb. "We'll be nearby."

"Will do," I said.

I got out of the car and shivered. The night was cold,

colder than it had been all year. That was okay, because it matched the icy pit in my stomach. Izzy had seemed distant at lunch today, and she barely looked at me. I couldn't tell if it was because she was avoiding me or because we had spent most of lunch listening to Sophia talk about how nervous she was to be spending Christmas with both of her parents, who hadn't seen each other in a few months.

Dandelion Square was packed and lively. Passersby clutching shopping bags went from shop to shop, and carolers dressed in Victorian clothing strolled the streets, while families posed for pictures in front of the town Christmas tree.

I ducked into Hollow Hall. Inside, tables were piled high with ribbons, wrapping paper, and bows. Grandma Bertie was heading up this year's Wrap-a-Thon, and she greeted me at the front, and said, "Hello, dear! I've got you at a table in the back with Izzy. Wait for someone to come by—it's ten dollars, no matter how many presents they have for you to wrap—and then let them pick the wrapping paper they want."

I passed the table where Sophia and Daisy were already working and waved. They both waved back glumly. They'd gotten stuck wrapping Mayor Franklin's presents—all twenty of them—while she chatted away on her cell phone.

"Where *were* you?" Izzy muttered when I sat down. She was finishing wrapping up what looked like a skateboard for Mike Harrison, the owner of Harrison's Hardware.

"Melanie was running late," I said.

After that, a line formed at our table and we couldn't talk. But I could tell from the stiffness in Izzy's shoulders that she was mad.

When there was a lull in the customers, I said, "Listen, I have something to tell you. I—"

"Have you been hanging out with Austin a lot?" She scraped the edge of her scissors against the ribbon she was holding so hard it curled into sparkly red spirals.

"Define 'a lot,'" I said.

She gave the ribbon another good scrape. "Violet— come on."

"Well, yeah. I guess we do sometimes, and we text a lot."

"Is that why you're never around when I call you on the walkie-talkie lately?"

"Um . . . maybe?"

"And you told him about your mom's list?" she asked, not looking at me.

"I told him when we were studying one day, and he

said he'd help." All of which was true, but I knew that wasn't exactly what she was asking me. "We have a class project together, and . . . I don't know, we just talk and . . . tell each other stuff."

"What kind of stuff?"

I shrugged. "I don't know. I guess I just talk to him about things I can't with anyone else."

"*What* things? What is so important that you can't talk to me about but you can talk to him about?"

"Just . . . things," I said desperately. "I talk to him about my mom, and Melanie and Olivia, and . . ." I took a deep breath. "Look, Izzy. I know you like him. But the thing is—I think I like him, too. I'm sorry if that makes you mad."

There, I said it.

Izzy had no shortage of people to talk to. Her dad took her kayaking all the time. Aunt Mildred and Grandma Bertie were always cooking breakfast for her; her sister Carolyn was seriously cool and nice. But it felt like Austin was the one person I could really talk to right now. Why did I have to stop hanging out with him because Izzy decided she needed yet another person on the long list of People Who Love Izzy?

Izzy looked like she'd love to take the present she

was wrapping and hit me over the head with it. "Seriously, Violet? You think I'm mad because you might have a crush on Austin Jackson?"

"Well . . . ," I said, feeling suddenly unsure, "yeah. Aren't you? You re-crush-dibbed him. You said you liked him."

"Yeah, I did—for, like, *four days*, until I saw him in English class, and he and Tyler Jones were acting totally immature. Which you would have known, if you'd bothered to ask—or been around when I tried calling you on the walkie."

"Okay," I said. Now I was really confused. If Izzy didn't like Austin, what exactly were we talking about right now? "I guess I just thought you'd be mad, and I really do like talking to him, and—"

"That's the problem, Violet!" she burst out. "You never want to talk to me—or Daisy or Sophia—even though we all know something's wrong. We ask you about your mom and Melanie, and you always say everything's just fine. But then you go behind my back and talk to Austin Jackson, of all people?"

"Because I can talk to him!" I yelled. "Because *you're* always too busy complaining about your mom. Because you think you have it so tough, having a mom who's difficult to be around. You have no idea how lucky you are!"

Izzy put her scissors down. She looked stricken.

"Izzy, I'm so sorry—" I began, but it was too late.

She had already stood up and walked away.

CHAPTER
31

IRIDESCENT

"Izzy, wait!" I called.

Izzy sprinted forward and slipped out of the hall, and I wondered if she was taking our friendship with her. There's a reason Mom always said if you can't say something nice, don't say anything at all. Nasty words can be like a jackhammer, busting up everything in their path. I knew my ugly words would pound at our friendship until it shattered into pieces, unless I took them back.

Stupid, stupid, stupid, I told myself as I stood up. I know Izzy has a temper, and I know not to lose mine around her. Once, she didn't speak to me for over a week because I was mad and called her weird—even though she'd just done something that was *totally* weird and that could've—and eventually *did*—get us into a ton of trouble.

Daisy and Sophia both hurried over. "What happened?" Sophia asked.

"I said something really stupid to Izzy, and now she's gone," I said. "I don't know what do to."

"Go after her," Sophia advised.

"Yeah," Daisy added. "We'll cover your table."

I grabbed my coat but immediately started shivering as soon as I went outside. It felt even colder than it had an hour ago. My breath came out in white puffs as I tried to figure out where Izzy would go. I decided to head for the Kaleidoscope Café—it was so cold, I thought maybe she'd go get a cup of hot chocolate. But when I walked up and looked through the café's window, I didn't see her. The only people I recognized inside were Austin and his parents. They were sitting in the big red booth in the front window, eating slices of cake.

Austin caught sight of me and said something to his parents before standing up and coming outside.

"It's colder than Frosty's butt out here," he said, jumping in place to warm himself.

"So your mom is back?" I said.

Austin nodded. "She loved the cooking school."

"When does she leave again?" I knew I needed to be finding Izzy, not talking to Austin right now. But I was already planning. I'd make a list of nice things to do for Austin on his first day without his mom: a pot of Stinky Soup, a nice card, and—

"Oh, no," Austin said quickly. "She's not leaving right away. She didn't like the nine-month program. But she loved the summer program."

"The summer program?" It shouldn't have mattered to me which program Mrs. Jackson liked. But still, I felt something like disappointment creeping into my bones.

"Yeah. She's going to go back for the summer program. And the best part? My dad decided he's way overdue for a long vacation. He has an uncle in New York, and we're going to stay with him for a month." He pumped his fist in the air. "It'll be the best summer vacation ever!"

As he finished speaking, something small and white drifted between us and came to rest on his nose. His eyes shot to it—making him look severely cross-eyed—and as more puffs fell around us, I understood:

Snow.

It hadn't snowed in Dandelion Hollow since I was five years old. And even then, it was only once, for five minutes in the middle of the night. But here it was falling; drifting all around us. Shyly at first, like an uninvited guest at a party where the welcome is uncertain, but picking up steam, taking over until all movement and all sound had come to a stop. All over the square, the people of Dandelion Hollow were staring up into the night sky. The Christmas carolers had ceased their singing, their melodies trailing off and spiraling upward into the night. A few of them, mouths hanging wide, were unintentionally catching flakes in their mouths. An iridescent snowflake came to rest in Austin's hair.

"Iridescent"—it means "shining with many different colors when seen from different angles."

I figured maybe that described how Austin and I felt about each other. From one angle, I thought Austin was cute and I liked talking to him. And if I was honest, I sort of liked being the person he talked to about his mom maybe leaving for nearly a year.

But now I was looking at things from a different angle. Sort of like that moment in a movie theater right after the film is over, and the lights come back on. You have to blink a few times before you see clearly enough to stand up and move on with your day.

As we stared at each other I felt my heart plummeting, which is just a gold star way of saying it was falling, and falling fast. I was happy for Austin, for his whole family. I really was. But I knew things were going to be different now. Maybe I'd never had a real crush on him. Maybe I'd just liked feeling like there was someone I could really talk to. But why, out of everyone I knew, had I picked Austin? If I really thought about it, I was pretty sure it was because I thought once his mom left for New York, we'd have a lot of things in common.

But Mrs. Jackson wasn't leaving her family behind. She was taking them with her.

"So, listen," Austin said, "our project is due in a few days, and I was thinking: Maybe I could handle the model of the pyramid and you could handle the essay? That would be the fastest way to get it done."

"Sure," I mumbled. "That sounds great." I felt so confused. I wasn't sure I still had a crush on Austin. And had *he* ever had a crush on *me*? He'd definitely flirted with me a couple times—but he didn't seem all that flirty right now. Or maybe like me, he got crushes all the time, but they never lasted more than a week or two.

"Sweet! Text you later?"

"Sure, text me later," I said.

After he went back inside, I drifted over to the town Christmas tree. The snow was already turning into a light rain—and a pang went through me when I realized I'd missed my chance to make a snow angel—and check off the hardest remaining thing on Mom's list. A few small snowflakes were still resting on the Christmas tree, but they were melting fast. A girl was standing in front of the tree with her back to me. Her combat boots were pink and sparkly, and the charm bracelet on her wrist matched my own: Izzy.

"Izzy!" I called as I ran over to her. "Izzy!"

She turned, caught a slippery patch of concrete, and went skidding across the square. I was about to tell her she looked like a combat-booted ice-skater—until her legs flew out from under her and she fell, striking her head on the ground.

CHAPTER
32

INDESTRUCTIBLE

Three days after Mom had told me she had cancer, I was standing outside her bedroom door, keeping watch while she took a nap. There was a knock at the front door, which I ignored. A few minutes later, Dad appeared. He had a hollowed-out, vacant expression in his eyes. "Izzy's here," he said. "She wants to know if you want to come outside?"

I looked over at the stair railing and imagined I could see Izzy downstairs, framed in our front doorway—her hair tangled in knots, her knees scraped up—waiting for me. Then I looked back at Mom's room; she was breathing heavily and looked pale.

"Tell her I'm busy." I didn't know it at the time, but

that was the beginning of Izzy and me not being friends anymore.

I looked back at Mom. "Please be okay," I said then.

"Please be okay," I said now, from the backseat of Melanie's minivan. I wasn't entirely sure how I'd gotten there. Izzy's dad must have been nearby and seen her fall, because all of a sudden he was at her side, and a short time later she was being loaded into an idling ambulance, its siren silently flaring and flashing. The next thing I knew, I was crouching in Dandelion Square, Melanie and Olivia standing over me, the glow of lamplight surrounding them like a halo.

"She's hurt," I'd said, and it sounded like my mouth was stuffed with rocks.

"What?" Melanie had said. "I didn't catch that."

I glanced over at Melanie's car; it was parked at an odd angle against the curb. The headlights were still on, and the backseat was piled high with shopping bags.

"She's hurt," I said again. Or did I just say it in my head?

"She doesn't look so good, Mom," Olivia whispered.

"I know. . . . Sir?" Melanie called to an elderly man who was standing near the lamp stand. "Can you tell me what happened?"

"A girl fell and hit her head," he had replied. "The chief of police's daughter, I think. Not the prodigy one—the younger one. Her dad decided to have her checked out at the hospital. Just to be safe."

Just to be safe. I heard his words, but I couldn't keep my mind from playing a game:

What If?

What if Izzy was really hurt? What if a doctor at the hospital talked to Izzy's dad and said the same six words that had once changed my whole life: *"We have something to tell you?"* Melanie had glanced at me, and I think she'd read everything I was thinking in my eyes, because she'd nodded her head, and when she spoke, she'd used her teacher voice. The Hammer's voice: "Olivia—call Mitch and tell him we'll be home late tonight. We're going to the hospital. Violet—" she held out her hand—"get up. It's time to go. Everything's going to be fine. We're going to see Izzy."

Please be okay, I thought again, as I stared out the car window. Everyone was silent as Melanie drove; the only sound was the whooshing of the windshield wipers.

"Violet?" Melanie glanced at me in the rearview mirror. "Are you okay? You look a little greenish. Do I need to pull the car over?"

"It's my fault," I said. "It's my fault she's in the hospital."

"Izzy fell because the streets are slippery tonight," Melanie said. "Not because of anything you did."

"That's not true." Quietly, I told her and Olivia all about hanging out with Austin, even after I thought Izzy liked him again. About ignoring Izzy's walkie-talkie calls, about telling Austin things I didn't tell Izzy. About not telling Izzy about my own crush on Austin. After I finished, they were both silent. I figured they thought I was a rotten friend.

"There was this boy I liked in the tenth grade," Melanie said softly. Through the rearview mirror I could see her smile. "Troy Wilkins. He was a football player, and a genuinely nice guy, or so I thought at the time. I was head over heels for him, and absolutely sure he liked me, too—until the next week, when he asked my best friend to the homecoming dance."

"Did she go to the dance with him?" Olivia asked, curious.

"She did. Oh, we had a terrible fight over it. Anyway, after the dance, the two of them became a couple—for about five weeks, until Troy dumped her for someone he'd met over Christmas break. But the damage was done. Our friendship was never the same after that, and gradually, we stopped being friends—all over a boy who wasn't a significant part of either of our lives." Melanie caught my eye again in the rearview mirror. "There are a lot of reasons why girls stop being friends, Violet—people change and drift apart. Don't let a boy be one of those reasons."

After Melanie parked the car in the hospital's lot, we went to the check-in counter, where the receptionist was happily gabbing away on the phone—apparently, her boyfriend was on thin ice, and had better get her something good for Christmas this year, *or else*. A line of irritated visitors stood in front of her desk, waiting for her to hang up. "Excuse me," Melanie said loudly. "But we're trying to locate my daughter's friend."

Olivia and I exchanged confused glances. Izzy and Olivia liked each other okay, but I didn't think they were actually friends.

The receptionist swiveled in her chair to glance at Melanie, but she kept talking; and after a few more seconds, Melanie ripped the received from her hands and snapped, "No one here cares about your taste in jewelry. Now get off the phone and help all of us."

The receptionist glared at Melanie, but wilted under the Hammer's stare. "What is your daughter's friend's name?" she asked in an almost-polite voice.

"Izzy Malone," Melanie answered.

"How does she *do* that?" I whispered to Olivia, who shrugged.

"It's an art," she whispered back. "She's like a magician."

But when I looked back at Melanie—jaw set, steely Hammer stare—she looked more like a warrior.

A warrior who was fighting for me.

We couldn't see Izzy right away; she was in the emergency room being examined by the doctor. It felt like we'd been sitting in the waiting room forever before her dad came out to see us.

"She's okay," he said immediately. "The doctor checked her out, and she's fine. No concussion."

"She's okay," I repeated, and let out a breath. I felt shaky on the inside, and I wondered if any of the others understood just how differently tonight could have gone. How one minute a person can be fine, and then the next they're just . . . not fine.

"Do you need me to call anyone for you?" Melanie asked him, and he shook his head.

"I already talked to Izzy's mom—she was in San Francisco with Carolyn for a music recital tonight—and they're driving back right now. The doctor said she doesn't have to stay overnight. I'm going to the cafeteria to get something to eat before I go back into her room. Violet, would you like to go look in on her?"

"Yes, please," I said, still feeling shaky.

Mr. Malone led us through the double doors to the emergency room. "She's over that way, just past the emergency exit," he said.

"I think Olivia and I will also go to the cafeteria," Melanie said. She placed a hand on my shoulder, and whispered, "Remember what we talked about in the car."

"I will," I said.

The three of them left, and I found Izzy in an alcove off to the side. She was lying under a blanket on a cot, surrounded by medical equipment.

"Hi," I said. "Are you okay?"

She nodded. "I'm fine. Apparently, I have a really hard head. It's indestructible!"

"Indestructible"—it can mean "unbreakable" or "durable." I guess that's what I wanted my friendship with Izzy to be like: Stronger than boys and secrets and crushes and the hurts of the world. Something that couldn't shatter into a million pieces.

"About what happened tonight," I said. "I figure Austin Jackson isn't worth us fighting over."

Izzy made a face. "You're just figuring that out *now*? I thought you were the smart one."

I laughed and sat next to her on the bed. "I guess I'm not always as smart as I think I am. And I'm sorry I didn't tell you I was hanging out with him." Slowly, I began to tell her about Mrs. Jackson's cooking school and bringing Austin a pot of Stinky Soup and ice-blocking and stringing popcorn garland and how it felt standing in the snow tonight, when he told me his mom wasn't going away for the year, and how it was a little bit like waking up from a dream.

"I'm not even sure I have a crush on him anymore," I finished. "In fact, I'm pretty sure I don't." That was all true, but even so, I felt a little sad and disappointed inside. Like going back to school in January and realizing all the fun and anticipation of the holidays were over and it was back to real life again.

"Can I ask you something?" Izzy sat up and looked at me tentatively. "Did you kiss him?"

"No," I said. "Definitely not."

"Good—would you have really wanted Austin's spit in your mouth?" Trust Izzy to turn kissing into the grossest thing in the world.

"Well, geez, Izzy, when you put it like that, I may never

kiss a boy ever in my life. Most of the time, we just talked about things." I took a deep breath. "Actually, we talked about my mom a lot." I wondered if I should apologize for talking to Austin instead of Izzy. But Izzy didn't look mad; she just seemed sort of sad and a little bit puzzled.

"A lot of the time it seems like you don't *want* to talk about your mom," she said. "But you can; you know that, right? You could talk to me—and Sophia and Daisy."

"I know. . . . I guess a lot of the time I feel like you guys wouldn't understand."

Izzy thought about that for a second. "I guess we wouldn't—couldn't—understand. But isn't that what friends are for? To help you try to talk through the things there's just no making sense of? Besides—" a touch of competitiveness entered her voice—"I am a *way* better listener than Austin." She flopped back on her bed. "Ugh. Austin's going to get an *A* on his Egyptian project because you're his partner. I seriously hope we have a lot of classes together next semester, Violet. If someone's going to benefit from your braintasticness, it should be *me*."

I had a feeling Austin and I wouldn't be hanging out quite as much once our project was finished. But something told me that if things had turned out differently, if Mrs. Jackson *had* moved away for most of next year, we would've continued on commiserating. I could have told him all about how to get used to living with just his dad, even if it was just for a short time. But that wasn't going to happen, and I figured it was okay. I guess what I really needed was just what Izzy had said: to start talking to the friends who were always there for me, no matter what. Sophia and Daisy, and especially Izzy.

"Let's make a pact," I said, and held out my hand. "From now on, we tell each other everything. . . . And do *not* spit in your hand, Izzy Malone," I added sternly, when it looked like she might. "That's not how I make deals."

Izzy laughed. "You're on." She took my hand and shook it.

Just then a doctor approached. "Hi, Izzy," he said. "I just need your dad to finish filling out a bit of paperwork, and then we'll get you out of here."

He was young. And cute. I mean, really, really cute.

"Thanks, Doctor," Izzy said, a giggle in her voice.

After he left, we looked at each other and smiled. And at the same time, we yelled, "Crush dibs!"

33

DANCING SNOW

Dear Mom,

I remember a long time ago how you once came bursting into my room late one night, the light from the hallway streaking in behind you, as you told me to Wake up! Get up! . . . There's snow! Let's make snow angels! *A flurry of untangling covers and hastily donned boots and jackets, and we rushed out into the night, me clinging to your soft hand. But the moment was already gone. The snow, brief as it was, had turned to misty rain.*

I still have that half-formed memory in my mind. But now I have another memory of snow: of watching it dance on the bridge of Austin's nose last night, the exact moment before I knew he wouldn't be my One, the way Dad was yours. And knew that I didn't even like him anymore. But I think maybe I know now why it's called a "crush" when you like a boy. Because when it ends, it feels like a piece of your heart gets crumpled up and ripped to pieces. Crushed.

That wasn't even the biggest news of the night. Izzy fell and hit her head pretty hard—she had to go to the hospital to make sure she didn't have a concussion. She's okay, though. Her dad let Sophia, Daisy, and me spend the night at her house. We stayed up nearly all night, and the three of them listened while I talked for a long time about you and Dad and Melanie, and how sometimes it's hard for me to understand why you couldn't have been one of the lucky ones who survived cancer. But I guess that's what good friends do: They listen to you and let you ask questions—even if they don't have the answers. They let you say all the words inside you, the good ones and the ugly ones, and they're still your friends afterward.

I've decided that's way better than keeping your words inside you all the time.

Love always,
Violet

P.S. When they heard that I had missed out on decorating the Christmas tree at home, Izzy made us take all the ornaments off her family's tree and we redecorated it. As I put the last ornament on, I could swear I heard you whisper, Merry Christmas.

CHAPTER 34

SISTERS?

"Pick a charm, any charm," I said to Olivia.

We were at Charming Trinkets, standing in front of the large display of bracelets and charms. Olivia had received her bracelet from Aunt Mildred yesterday. Then this morning, I'd told her we were going to the jewelry shop so I could buy her Christmas present: matching charms for the two of us to put on our bracelets.

"Shouldn't we pick them out together?" Olivia said. "There are so many of them."

"Okay . . . what about this?" I picked up a tiny dictionary charm.

Olivia rolled her eyes. "You study too much; it's kind

of boring." She found a schoolhouse charm. "What about this one?"

Now I rolled my eyes. "*You* spend way too much time in school meetings. Totally boring," I said.

We smiled at each other, then Olivia said, "Oh, look at that one! That's it!" She unhooked a red gummy-bear charm from the display rack, and held it up. "What do you think?"

"That's definitely the one," I agreed.

The charm had meaning for both of us because we were now spending a lot of time plotting to make sure Melanie and Dad—M&M, we both called them now, since it was so much easier than saying "Mom and Mitch" or "Dad and Melanie"—didn't discover our secret candy stash. Melanie was using the fact that I was a vegetarian as an excuse to make everyone in the house eat as healthy as possible. It was so bad, I was considering telling her I was changing my eating habits. In the meantime, though, Olivia and I were pooling our spare change and stocking up on our favorites from Harrison's Hardware: licorice and gummy bears.

"Merry Christmas," I said after I'd paid for the charms.

"Should we wait until Christmas morning to put them on?" Olivia was staring longingly at the golden chain on her wrist; it was empty since she hadn't had her first meeting with her friends yet.

"No," I said. "Let's put them on now."

Olivia frowned. "I feel like we need to earn it, some-how. That's how it works, right?"

"Right." I thought for a second. "Well . . . we've sur-vived living together for nearly a month now. I'd say we've more than earned it."

Olivia grinned. "That is so true."

We each held the tiny gummy bears in the palms of our hands. "We have earned our charm," I said solemnly, and we began hooking them onto our bracelets.

"Why, what lovely bracelets," said a lady who was brows-ing through the shop. "Are you two sisters?" she asked.

Olivia and I stared at each other. Neither of us quite knew how to answer the question.

"Well . . . ," I began, just as Olivia said, "Um . . ."

"I guess you could say we're . . . friends, right?" Olivia looked at me.

"Right," I agreed quickly. "We're friends."

"Friends"—It means "one who is attached to another by feelings of affection or esteem." That sounded about right. I guess "friends" could work for today.

But I could also imagine a day not too far away when "sisters" might work, too.

SECOND-CHANCE FAMILY

"Violet, could you come into the kitchen, please?" Melanie called.

"Be right there," I called back, and hauled myself off the couch. It was the Wednesday before Christmas; winter break had already started, and I was hanging out in the living room, watching a movie with Joey and Olivia. In a couple hours, I was supposed to meet up with Izzy, Daisy, and Sophia at the Kaleidoscope Café to exchange our Secret Santa gifts.

"What's up?" I said when I entered the kitchen. Melanie was sitting at the table, and she gestured for me to sit next to her. "I need to talk to you," she said.

"Okay." I slid into the chair beside her. Mentally, I reviewed everything that I'd said and done over the last few days, but I couldn't come up with anything that would warrant a serious heart-to-heart. *Remember to try*, I repeated to myself. It was my new mantra.

"Mantra"—it means "a statement or slogan repeated constantly," and I'd been constantly trying to make a better effort this week: going out to breakfast with Melanie, Joey, and Olivia yesterday; finishing up one last round of Christmas shopping the day before; going ice-skating with them last night—it wasn't as bad as I thought it would be.

Melanie pressed her fingertips together and took a deep breath. "I'm sorry."

"*You're* sorry?" I repeated, surprised. "For what?"

She didn't answer right away. She looked out the window, and said, "I don't think I've handled our first month together the best way I could've. I don't know if your dad told you any of this, but . . . things weren't ever that good between my parents and me. I'll spare you the details, but let's just say the day I married Joey and Olivia's dad, I thought I'd been rescued. Of course, it didn't take me too long to realize I'd jumped out of one hard situation and right into another. But I'd longed so much for a family of my own that I was determined to make it work, and, for a while at least, it did work. Of course, it takes two people to make a marriage succeed. . ." She trailed off, then seemed to shake away bad memories. "When I met your dad, it was like all the hurt places inside me healed. Not completely. I don't know if any one person can completely heal another; sometimes I think that's solely the work of the Divine. But we were two broken pieces, and somehow our jagged edges fit right together. Anyway, I guess what I'm saying is: I've been so intent on doing things right this time around, on trying to make sure we had the perfect family Christmas, I didn't stop to think that maybe you needed something different. Maybe you needed time with your friends. I'm sorry I haven't seen how important your charm club is, or how much you've needed Daisy, Izzy, and Sophia, and—"

She broke off when my phone pinged; it was a text from Austin:

I have an epic surprise for you!

"Go ahead and answer him," Melanie said. When I looked up, I saw that she'd read the text. And she was smiling.

Weird.

What is it? I texted back quickly. I'm meeting Izzy, Daisy, and Sophia at the Kaleidoscope soon.

That's what YOU think!

Whatever, Austin. I'm busy.

To my surprise, Austin had still been texting me. Not nearly as much as before, and whatever crush we may have had on each other, it had definitely gone away. But I was okay with that; I guess when I thought back over the last month I just wanted someone to understand what it was like to have a Terrible Beautiful Ache inside you that you knew wouldn't ever completely go away.

But maybe Melanie, Olivia, and Joey, along with Dad, *did* understand that. I guess in a way, all five of us had been left behind by someone we loved. We were the lonely left-overs, and somehow we were going to have to figure out how to weave ourselves into a new pattern that had space enough for all of us.

Maybe that's what Melanie had been trying to do all this time, moving and shifting things around, trying to make space for the shape that our new family would take. Because we *were* a family, I realized. A second-chance family. Not the one you thought you'd have, but the one offered to you after some of the worst things in the world had happened to you.

"I shouldn't be long at the Kaleidoscope today," I said. "Afterward, I can come home and the four of us can do something." Sophia had talked about having the Charm Girls over for dinner tonight, but actually, the thought of hanging out with just Melanie, Olivia, and Joey seemed kind of fun. "Dad gets lonely, working so many hours in December," I added. "Sometimes Mom and I would bring him dinner and we'd hang out in the shop with him." It felt strange mentioning Mom to Melanie, mentioning my old life, but I knew it was part of weaving together a new pattern. "Anyway," I said, "we could bring him dinner."

"That sounds like a great idea," Melanie said. She slid a furniture catalog toward me and pointed to a wooden table. "Your dad and I purchased this yesterday—it will be delivered tomorrow, just in time for Christmas." The table was circular and rustic-looking. And best of all, it had five chairs.

"There is always a place for you at my table, Violet," Melanie said. "I'm sorry if I haven't made that clear this last month. And if you and your friends and Aunt Mildred need a place for your Charm Girl meetings, there are five seats here—it's exactly enough."

"You're right," I said, smiling. "It's exactly enough."

"Mom! Violet!" Olivia yelled from the living room. "Come look out the front window!"

"In a minute!" I yelled back.

"Actually," Melanie said. "I really think you should go look out the window."

She smiled mysteriously, her eyes twinkling, just as Austin sent me another text that read:

We're here!

I raced to the living room just as the doorbell rang. I flung open the door; Izzy, Sophia, and Daisy stood on the front porch dressed in thick coats, hats, and gloves.

"Surprise!" they yelled. Behind them, three long trucks packed with snow were parked in front of our house. Dad and Chief Malone were just exiting the first truck, while Grandpa Caulfield and Scooter McGee sat in the second truck. In front of the third truck, Mr. Jackson was handing Austin a shovel. As I watched, Grandma Bertie's minivan pulled up behind the last truck. She, Aunt Mildred, Mrs. Ramos, and Izzy's mom got out of the car and started passing out cups of coffee to everyone.

"What's going on?" I asked.

"The four of you are going to make snow angels," Melanie said behind us. I turned, and she was smiling. "I believe, 'make a snow angel' was on your mother's list? Earlier today everyone got the trucks and headed up the highway until they found some snow. They pulled over and started loading up. We're going to turn our front yard into a winter wonderland!"

Dad, Austin, Mrs. Ramos, Mr. Jackson, and both Izzy's parents started shoveling snow from the trucks onto the yard. Joey went running from the house and promptly began building a snowman.

My throat closed up tight at the thought that so many people had been working hard to help me accomplish the last thing on Mom's list—and to do it in a completely crazy way. Word must have spread, and before you knew it people were lining up to help. Mom would have said that's the good kind of gossip, and one of the best things about living in a small town.

Olivia and I ran upstairs to get our snow things. Izzy poked her head into my room as I was tugging on my boots. "Hey—I just want you to know, Melanie put this whole thing together. She pulled me aside in class right before school let out and asked if there was anything she could do to help you check an item off your mom's list."

"She did?" I said, and a funny feeling went through my chest.

Izzy nodded seriously. "About gave me a heart attack—I thought I was in trouble again."

"In trouble, for what?" I asked.

"Uh, nothing," Izzy said quickly. "I mean, I didn't do anything. Anyway, I told her how you hadn't been able to make a snow angel. I figured she was just going to take you to the snow one day. But then she called my parents a couple days ago with this crazy idea. She said . . . " Izzy's eyes grew tentative. "She said she thought maybe you'd want to make snow angels with Daisy, Sophia, and me."

"She was right," I said, and smiled.

Back downstairs, Melanie was in the kitchen, unpacking a bag of multicolored marshmallows, caramel sauce, peppermint sticks, and ribbon candy.

"What's all this for?" I asked.

"It's a make-your-own hot-chocolate bar," she answered. "I'll have it ready after you guys are finished."

"Thanks, Melanie," I said, and I think she knew I meant for more than just the hot chocolates.

While we waited for Dad and the others to finish shoveling, Izzy, Daisy, Sophia, and I headed to the living room to quickly exchange our Secret Santa gifts.

"I want to go first!" Daisy said. She held out a sloppily wrapped package, yelled "Merry Christmas!" and handed it to . . . Sophia. "Surprise! I'm your Secret Santa!"

Sophia definitely looked surprised. "I'm your Secret Santa, too," she said, handing Daisy a box wrapped with pretty pale-pink paper. While they unwrapped their gifts, Izzy and I smiled at each other; that meant we had drawn each other's names.

Somehow it seemed fitting.

"Oh, wow, Sophia, this is amazing." Daisy lifted Sophia's gift out of the box. It was a notepad that flipped open from the top. It was made out of brown leather and had Daisy's name embossed in gold at the bottom.

"Cool! Thanks, Sophia."

"You're welcome. I thought you could use it to write down your notes for your news articles."

Sophia's present was a necklace with a dandelion pendant. "It's so you'll think of us all back here in Dandelion Hollow while you're spending Christmas in San Francisco," Daisy said.

"Okay, it's our turn now!" Izzy said. She handed me a red bag. "Open it!" Inside was a new journal. A purple one. But on the inside, Izzy had cut out different words and pasted them here and there all over the pages. On the first page she'd pasted: "wondrous," "Christmas," and "friendship." It must have taken her hours—and I know Izzy can't stand to do crafts.

"Where did you get all these words?" I asked.

"I cut them all out of my dictionary," Izzy said proudly.

"Don't look so shocked, Violet. Not everyone is married to theirs, the way you are. It looked to me like you were running out of pages to write your word lists on in your old journal, so I thought you could use a new one."

"Thank you," I said. "I love it."

"No problem. I think you should start a new list: People I Like the Most—and my name should be at the top!"

"Thanks, Izzy," I said, and gave her my present: a big box wrapped in candy-cane paper.

"Ooh, the biggest one is for me!" she squealed, and we all laughed.

"I hope you like it," I said as she tore into it. Once she opened the box, she became still. "Wow, Violet. This is amazing."

"What is it?" Daisy said, craning her neck to see. "The suspense is killing me."

Izzy lifted up a pair of sparkly camouflage combat boots—an exact match to the pink ones she loved so much, except these ones were purple. It had cost me every single dollar I'd saved of my allowance, and once Grandma Barnaby sent me her annual Christmas check, I was going to have to turn most of it over to Dad to pay him back, but I didn't care. It was totally worth it to see the smile that spread across Izzy's face.

The front door opened then, and Dad called, "We're finished! You can all come out now!"

Everyone else was already standing on the porch when Izzy, Daisy, Sophia, and I made it outside. "Wow," I said. "Thank you so much. This is amazing." It really did look like a winter wonderland. They'd brought back enough snow to blanket the entire front yard.

"Before we get started," Dad began, "someone here would like to make a special announcement."

"What's going on?" I heard Sophia whisper to Izzy, who replied, "No idea."

But from the way all the adults were smiling mischievously, it was clear they knew exactly what was going on. Except for Aunt Mildred, who looked confused.

Scooter stepped into the middle of the porch, where we'd all formed a circle. He took a deep breath, and right there in front of everyone, he turned to Aunt Mildred and slowly sank to one knee.

"Mildred Arlene Percival!" he announced in a loud voice, "I've got a question for you."

Everyone was silent, except for Daisy, who said, "Who's Mildred Arlene Percival?"

"Duh," Izzy answered, looking pointedly at Aunt Mildred.

"Oh, right," Daisy said quickly.

"You told me you didn't like the word 'boyfriend,'" Scooter continued, and produced a small black box. "Well, what about the word 'husband'? Do you like that one better?" He opened the box, revealing a diamond ring glittering against black velvet.

"That's the most moving thing I've ever heard," Sophia whispered.

Aunt Mildred looked pretty moved—although whether she was moved to kiss Scooter or throttle him, I couldn't tell. She looked around at all the smiling faces—especially at the adults, none of whom seemed surprised at all. "How dare you—did you actually"—she sputtered—"Do you mean to tell me you already told all these people you were going to propose?"

Scooter didn't look even a bit ashamed. "I did indeed! I knew I had to get the blessing of all your people before I could take the liberty of asking for your hand in marriage. I'm here to tell you, I've gotten them. A million blessings—all I need is the biggest one of them all. Say yes, Milly. Please."

Aunt Mildred stared at the ring and hesitated.

"Oh, for heaven's sake, Mildred," Grandma Bertie said. "It's freezing out here—say yes before the girls become senior citizens themselves."

Aunt Mildred didn't seem to have heard; her eyes had taken on a faraway quality. I was sure she was thinking of her first husband and the car crash that took him away from her all those years ago and how differently her life had gone ever since.

"Say yes," I spoke up. "He's your second-chance family." I clapped a hand over my mouth, because I knew you weren't supposed to say anything while you were watching someone propose to someone else. But I also knew I was right. Everyone surrounding us, they weren't just Aunt Mildred's people, they were *my* people, too. And I knew we were both so lucky to have them.

"What?" Aunt Mildred said, turning to me. "What did you say?"

"Well . . . ," I said slowly, looking at Melanie. "We're all born into a family—but sometimes bad things happen, and if you're lucky, you get a second chance. A chance to create another family."

"A second-chance family," Aunt Mildred murmured. "I like it."

"I've loved you since I was a boy, Mildred," Scooter said. "Now that I'm an old man, I love you still. Will you marry me?"

"I will," Aunt Mildred whispered.

Everyone broke into boisterous applause as Scooter placed the ring on her finger.

"Boisterous"—it can mean "very noisy or active in a lively way." Right now I was feeling lively and active, and I needed to do something before my heart jumped clear out of my chest. I grabbed Izzy's and Sophia's hands. Sophia reached for Daisy, and the four of us went running down the porch steps.

"Come join us!" I called to Olivia over my shoulder.

The five of us made a line. "On three," I said. "One . . . two . . . three!" We all flopped onto our backs and began moving our arms and legs back and forth—creating a line of snow angels. Cold from the snow was seeping into my back, but warmth was spreading through my heart. Everyone here, Melanie and Joey and Olivia and the Charm Girls and their families, they were my second-chance family, and I couldn't help but wonder if Mom had sent them all to me, just when I needed them.

As I stared up at the December sky, Izzy's and Sophia's fingertips brushing mine as we made our snow angels, it felt like that thin wall of glass that always separated me from everyone else began to shift and stretch, until it broke apart and dissolved, and was no more.

36

NEW PATTERNS

Dear Mom,

Christmas was five days ago, and I'm not going to lie,
it was hard. The Terrible Beautiful Ache was wrapping
around me like a sad blanket while we all opened
presents, and just when I didn't think I could take
it anymore, I glanced up at the fireplace mantle and
noticed someone had moved aside Melanie's collection
of nutcrackers and put a picture of you up there,
and it made me feel better. Melanie took down all the
Christmas decorations this morning, but I noticed she
kept your picture up there. That made me happy.

This is going to sound strange, but sometimes I wonder, if life had turned out differently, would you and Melanie have been friends?

We've made some new patterns: Every morning, Olivia, Joey, and I have been watching TV on the couch, and passing our secret bag of candy back and forth under a blanket when Melanie isn't looking. It was fun until Dad called the three of us the Lazy Lumps the other morning and said if we didn't get out of the house, he'd give us all chores to do. That got us all moving pretty fast, so we went over to Austin's house, and the two of us took Olivia and Joey and Izzy ice-blocking down Poppy Hill.

Another new pattern is that Melanie moved your old record player into the living room, and I can play your records whenever I want. Olivia doesn't think that's fair, because she's not allowed to play her music downstairs anytime she wants, but Melanie said that's just too bad because Olivia's music gives her a headache. We've been listening to Ella Fitzgerald and Louis Armstrong at night after dinner. I guess Gray Christmas actually hasn't been as gray as I thought it would be.

I guess in some ways, it's been wondrous.

I finally told Melanie all about the Terrible Beautiful Ache and Gray Christmas, and she said she hopes next year will be even better. She says she's already planning for a brighter Christmas. Beige Christmas, she called it. I thought that sounded sort of nerdy, but also sort of funny. And sweet.

I think what I'm trying to say is, I'm going to be okay. Maybe one day, I'll just feel grateful for the Christmases I had with you, instead of sad for all the ones we didn't get to have together. I still like to think that you're watching me, and I hope you're proud of me.

I've decided to keep writing you, because it makes me feel like you're still here, even if I can't see you.

Like maybe you've just walked into another room to put an album on your record player, and at any moment, I'll catch a glimpse of you again.

Love always,
Violet

ACKNOWLEDGMENTS

Of all the books I've written, this has been the most challenging, and it would not have been possible without the heroic efforts of my amazing editor, Alyson Heller. Alyson: Thank you for all your fantastic revision notes. Thank you, too, for always partnering with me on the vision that I have for my books, and then going out of your way to help me make them the very best they can be.

To Stefanie Wass, my critique partner and friend: Thank you so much for your fantastic editorial eye. This book is so much stronger because of your input. One day our paths will cross and we will finally meet in person!

To Kerry Sparks, my Agent of Awesome: None of this would ever be possible without you!

To Deanna Bosley, Christina Edwards, Lora Knopf, Deana Lewis, Dorothy Poole, Christina Sahota, Donelle Swain, and everyone else who joins our Wine and Appetizer Nights: Thank you for being a refuge where we can chat about everything from faith to parenting to books to all the vacations we daydream about taking together one day.

To Suzette Leger: Thank you for always going so far out of your way to encourage me and make me feel like a rockstar.

To Rose Cooper and Shannon Dittemore: Thanks for putting up with me on our "writing days" when I spend most of the time procrastinating and trying to distract you!

To Kristin Dwyer, Adrienne Sandvos, Joanna Rowland and Jessica Taylor the fearless leader of Team NorCal, and the rest of our crew, I don't know what I would do without having a community of writers like you guys. Go Team NorCal!

To the Journey Girls: Annie Chin, Carrie Diggs, Ruth Gallo, Cara Lane, and Sarah Mahieu: You are my soul sisters, and I am so lucky to have you. Thank you for being a place where we can say all the words inside us—the good ones and the hard ones—and still be there for each other.

To the Allen, Carroll, Lundquist and Winkler families, thank you for all your constant encouragement and support.

And finally, to Ryan Lundquist, who taught our boys how to go ice-blocking, and who once drove up Highway 50 to find snow so he could turn our drought-stricken front yard into a Winter Wonderland, I am so glad we get to do life together. You are truly my One.

And thank you to God. This world you created is truly wondrous. Thank you for all the amazing people you've put in my life.

Turn the page for a look at

THE CHARMING LIFE OF
IZZY MALONE

CHAPTER
1

The bracelet and the first charm appeared the day I punched Austin Jackson in the nose. I didn't mean to slug him. His face just got in my way. It was a bruising end to a disastrous first month in middle school.

You know that kid in class that everyone secretly (and not-so-secretly) thinks is weird? The one people laugh and point at behind their back, the one who gets picked last in gym class, the one you wish you hadn't gotten stuck with for a science partner?

At Dandelion Middle School, that kid is me, Izzy "Don't Call Me Isabella" Malone.

Truthfully, my slide into loserdom started in elementary

school and was pretty much an established fact by the time sixth grade started last month. It's partly because my mouth often has a mind of its own. But I think it's also because there are a bazillion other things I'd rather do than talk about boys, clothes, and makeup, and I refuse to wear strappy sandals and short skirts.

(If you ever catch me wearing strappy sandals or a short skirt, you have my permission to kick my butt.)

I *do* like skirts, though. Really long, colorful ones I get from Dandelion Thrift. I like to wear them with my camouflage combat boots.

I call the look Camohemian.

"I don't understand how it could be locked," Ms. Harmer, my English teacher said, tugging on the door of our classroom. "Fifteen minutes ago it was open."

"Does this mean class is cancelled?" I asked. Our class was held in an outdoor portable. The day was chilly but sunny, and being stuck indoors writing another round of horrible haikus was the last thing I wanted to do.

"No, Isabella—"

"Izzy," I said.

"—that is definitely *not* what that means. Everyone wait here while I go to the teacher's lounge to look for my keys. Lauren, you're in charge while I'm gone."

Lauren Wilcox smiled, all angelic-like. "I will." After Ms. Harmer left, Lauren's smile pulled back, like a beast baring its fangs. "You heard her. *I'm* in charge."

Students clumped off into their cliques. Being the class outcast, I am thoroughly cliqueless, and normally I'd sit by myself. But today I was planning to change all that.

Lauren and her friends claimed a grassy patch of sunlight—kicking out a couple other girls who'd gotten there first. I stared at them and squared my shoulders, preparing myself to do some major strappy-sandal smooching up. Lauren and her crew are the sixth-grade members of the Dandelion Paddlers, a competitive after-school rowing club. Lauren's family owns the aquatic center on Dandelion Lake, and you need to get in good with Lauren if you want to be a Paddler.

I learned that the hard way last summer during Paddler tryouts. I thought the fact that I was a great rower would be enough. There were four open spots, and they all went to Lauren's friends—even though I came in fourth during the timed heats. The last spot went to Stella Franklin, who had somehow managed to become BFFs with Lauren over the summer. I'm guessing the fact that Stella can kiss butt faster than a frog can catch flies has something to do with it.

But I wasn't about to give up. Being on the Paddlers is a big deal in Dandelion Hollow; when my dad was my age he was on the boys' team. He's taken me rowing for years, and we trained for tryouts all summer. Dandelion Lake is my favorite place in the world. I love being on the open water, where the only thing I feel is the wind in my hair, and words like "odd" and "strange" blow away like dead leaves on a blustery autumn day.

Lauren's locker is right next to mine, and this morning I took an extra-long time loading up my backpack so I could listen while she told her friends they were one Paddler short since Emily Harris moved away last week. I figured now was my chance.

"Hi," I said, plunking down next to Lauren. "It's weird Ms. Harmer can't find her keys, right?" I took the headphones from my iPod out of my skirt pocket and twirled them around, like I was bored and just making conversation.

Lauren blinked at me like I was a species she didn't recognize.

"Um, excuse me," Stella Franklin said. "What makes you think you can just sit here?"

It's a free country, is what I wanted to say. "I want to join you" is what I blurted instead.

"*You* want to join *us*?" said another of Lauren's friends. A husky blond girl who was wearing a chunky red headband over her ponytail.

"I mean, I want to join the Paddlers." I looked at Lauren. "I know you have an open spot, and last summer at tryouts I finished ahead of her." I jabbed my finger at Stella, who swelled up like a puffer fish.

"You did not! We tied."

"Nope," I said, twirling my headphones. "I beat you by three-tenths of a second."

Lauren leaned back and looked me up and down. I sat up straight, trying to appear taller. I'm pretty short, but what I lack in size I make up for in won't-quit-till-I-die persistence.

"I only have winners on my team," she said.

"I'm a winner," I said. Only my voice squeaked a little, and "winner" came out "wiener."

"Did you just call yourself a wiener?" Headband Girl asked.

Everyone laughed, and I counted silently to ten, because my patience was all puckered out.

"I think if you saw me paddle again," I said, crossing my legs, "then you'd realize I'm much better than—"

"What are *those*?" Stella interrupted, poking at my combat boots. "Those are the ugliest things I've ever seen. Don't you know boys don't like to get up close and personal with girls who wear boots like that?" She poked me again.

"You keep running your mouth," I snapped, smacking her hand away, "and these boots will get up close and personal with your face."

Darn it! The mouth strikes again!

Lauren directed her gaze to Headband Girl, who seemed to take it as a silent command. She snatched away my headphones and flung them in the air. They circled once in the breeze before landing on an overhanging branch of a nearby tree. Then, one by one, Lauren, Stella, Headband, and the rest of them stood up and left in a line of ponytail-swinging nastiness, leaving me sitting alone, while the rest of the class watched me, waiting to see what I would do.

Yeah, stuff like this is pretty much why I think middle school stinks.

Let's just pause for a moment to consider my options. I could:

> a. cry, which would only convince them I
>   didn't belong on their team.
> b. kick Headband's butt into the next
>   county. (Or try to, anyway. It's hard to

appear threatening to someone who has
biceps the size of Nebraska.)

  c. get my headphones back.

Here's the key to surviving as a middle school out-cast: Pretend you don't care. Pretend you have such great self-esteem that everything just rolls off your back. Most important:

Don't show weakness. Ever.

I chose option C. I have a thing for trees, and I'd wanted to climb this particular one for a while. I eat lunch under it every day, on account of the fact that the cafeteria usually smells like burnt burritos.

Plus, it's not like I have anyone to eat with, anyway.

I stood up and stretched. A skip, a hop, and a shimmy later, I was scrambling up the trunk.

"Go, Izzy!" shouted Austin Jackson, who, at the moment, still had a bruise-free face. A few other kids started cheering; Lauren and the Paddlers were already forgotten.

See what I mean? Pretend you don't care. Works like a charm.

I braced my hands against the rough trunk. The star-shaped leaves were the color of a fiery peach, and they whispered in the breeze. The air smelled sharp and crisp, like shiny red apples, and I breathed deep, enjoying being a little bit closer to the sky.

"Toad Girl is crazy," Stella was saying down below. I pretended not to hear. I also pretended I didn't know that was what most of the kids at Dandelion Middle called me. Stella the Terrible and I went to elementary school together and she gave me the nickname at her fourth-grade slumber party, when I put a toad in her sleeping bag. (I swear, that girl can howl like a werewolf on a full moon.)

I hadn't meant to do it. I just got bored watching everyone else test out Stella's lip gloss collection, and I started playing with her brother's sand toad, Count Croakula. I guess I must have lost him. But Stella swore up and down I'd done it on purpose, so I wasn't invited to her birthday party last year. I wasn't invited to a lot of birthday parties last year.

Turns out, most girls would rather put on lip gloss than play with sand toads.

"Come down from there! You'll get us all in trouble!" Stella was now standing under the tree. Lauren must have dispatched her to keep me in line. "Come on. Ms. Harmer will be back any minute."

"Leave Izzy to her solitary pursuits," said Violet Barnaby, who liked to use fancy words. She was sitting off to the side by herself, scribbling in a glittery purple journal. "Ms. Harmer won't find her keys in the teachers' lounge."

"How do you know that?" Stella demanded.

"Because I have them right here." Violet produced a key ring and jingled it.

The class gave a collective gasp, as Violet was known for being an A student who never got in trouble. I took the opportunity to climb up the branch. Slowly, I inched my way across it, where my headphones dangled in the breeze.

"Hey, Toad Girl!" called Tyler Jones. "Think fast!"

He lobbed an orange at me. It missed by a few feet and Austin said, "Tyler, you moron! Get out from under there. . . . I said, *Get Out!*"

"Ouch! All right, all right. I'm going!"

I kept inching forward, and stretched my fingers out to get the headphones. From up here I had a good view of several clusters of maple trees, which in late September were all colored in shades of gold and red and orange. A part of me wished I could stay up here forever, away from the middle school mean girls, who circled like sharks below me. I picked a few leaves and stuck them in my pocket, so I could paste them into my leaf collection later.

"What's going on?" came Ms. Harmer's voice. "Is someone up there?"

Startled, I lost my balance and fell. I caught myself on the branch and swung—gymnast style—through the air, landing right in front of Ms. Harmer.

"Ta-da!" I said, throwing my hands in the air.

A few kids applauded, but Ms. Harmer's face turned purple. "Go to the office. Now!"

As I walked away, I heard Stella say, "Excuse me, Ms. Harmer? You should probably send Violet to the office too. After all, she's the one who stole your keys."

CHAPTER
2

Coco Martin, my guidance counselor, was unimpressed with my daredevil skills. She tossed me a tube of ointment and a box of Band-Aids. "Clean yourself up," she said, gesturing to some cuts and scrapes on my arms. Then she went back to decorating her office for the fall. On her desk sat piles of tiny pumpkins and colorful ears of corn.

"Someone's grouchy today," I said, rubbing ointment onto my elbow. "Can't you be a little nicer?"

Coco grunted and stuck a pumpkin on her bookcase. "Consider yourself lucky. The only reason you're not in Principal Chilton's office right now is because Ms. Harmer decided stealing keys is a bigger offense than climbing trees. . . . And how many more times am I going to have to tell you not to put your feet up on my desk?"

"I don't know," I said. "How many more times do you think I'll get sent to your office?"

"That's a mystery to me. You've only been here a month, and I think you already hold the school record. It's been—what?—two days since I last saw you? When you kicked Tyler Jones in the shin."

"*That* was totally not my fault. Tyler called me a weirdo and a waste of space."

"'Sticks and stones may break my bones, but names can never hurt me.' It's a saying," Coco said. "Ever heard of it?"

"You know what? Now that you mention it, I think I have!" I nearly sprained my eyeballs, I was trying so hard not to roll them. Words are a weapon, and rotten kids like Tyler Jones get a free pass when it comes to using them, because the marks they leave are invisible. Why don't more adults realize that?

"Tyler trips me every day in class," I pointed out. "He just never gets caught. He hates being my science partner."

"Be that as it may, you need to stop showing up in my office. . . . You know, your sister spent three whole years here, and I don't think I ever even met her."

"Right," I said, feeling the familiar twinge I got whenever Carolyn the Great was mentioned. "But you know your day is always more interesting when me and my sparkling personality make an appearance in it."

Coco pressed her lips together, like she was trying not to smile. "Maybe so. *But,*"—her voice became stern—"sparkling personality or not, I still have to send a note home. School policy and all."

Coco scribbled on the incident report form I was intimately acquainted with and handed it to me just as the bell rang. "Have your parents sign this and bring it back to me," she said.

"I know the drill," I answered, shoving the note into my skirt pocket.

On the walk home from school I passed Violet, who lives in my neighborhood. Violet and I used to be best friends, the kind that played together at lunch and every day after school in my treehouse. Sometimes we'd pretend we were secret CIA agents, or sometimes we'd throw sand at each other and pretend it was fairy dust. But after Violet's mom got sick, and especially after Mrs. Barnaby passed away, Violet never wanted to play.

I considered slowing down to say hi, but Violet was hunched forward, her red peacoat fluttering in the wind as she stomped through a pile of fallen leaves. She didn't look like she wanted company. I bet she'd gotten into a heap load of trouble for stealing Ms. Harmer's keys, and I felt a little bad, because maybe Stella wouldn't have told on her if I hadn't climbed the tree.

I sped up and came upon a group of kids who were laughing. "Hey, Toad Girl!" a boy said as I passed. "Caught any flies lately?" Something small pinged off my shoulder.

"Dude, she *looks* like a toad," said another boy, as everyone laughed. "Ribbit, ribbit."

Sticks and stones, I told myself.

I felt the ping again and saw a yellow candy corn bounce off my arm and onto the ground—they were throwing them at me. I picked it up and yelled, "Thanks for the snack!" before popping it in my mouth and running ahead.

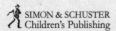